BUSHWHACKED!

The first bullet struck Long Henry in the chest. Another slug slammed into his side, spinning him around, dropping him to the boardwalk.

From across the intersection appeared the dim outline of a man holding a Winchester, and the sound of another shell being levered into its breech.

"Nice night for a killing," the man said, flashing a golden smile, and in that brief shock-filled moment the marshal of Waco knew the next bullet was going to slam into his head . . .

VISIT THE WILD WEST
with Zebra Books

SPIRIT WARRIOR   (1795, $2.50)
by G. Clifton Wisler
The only settler to survive the savage Indian attack was a little boy. Although raised as a red man, every man was his enemy when the two worlds clashed — but he vowed no man would be his equal.

IRON HEART   (1736, $2.25)
by Walt Denver
Orphaned by an Indian raid, Ben vowed he'd never rest until he'd brought death to the Arapahoes. And it wasn't long before they came to fear the rider of vengeance they called . . . *Iron Heart*.

THE DEVIL'S BAND   (1903, $2.25)
by Robert McCaig
For Pinkerton detective Justin Lark, the next assignment was the most dangerous of his career. To save his beautiful young client's sisters and brother, he had to face the meanest collection of hardcases he had ever seen.

KANSAS BLOOD   (1775, $2.50)
by Jay Mitchell
The Barstow Gang put a bullet in Toby Markham, but they didn't kill him. And when the Barstow's threatened a young girl named Lonnie, Toby was finished with running and ready to start killing.

SAVAGE TRAIL   (1594, $2.25)
by James Persak
Bear Paw seemed like a harmless old Indian — until he stole the nine-year-old son of a wealthy rancher. In the weeks of brutal fighting the guns of the White Eyes would clash with the ancient power of the red man.

Available wherever paperbacks are sold, or order direct from the Publisher. Send cover price plus 50¢ per copy for mailing and handling to Zebra Books, Dept. 2155, 475 Park Avenue South, New York, N.Y. 10016. Residents of New York, New Jersey and Pennsylvania must include sales tax. DO NOT SEND CASH.

ROBERT KAMMEN
LONG HENRY

ZEBRA BOOKS
KENSINGTON PUBLISHING CORP.

ZEBRA BOOKS

are published by

Kensington Publishing Corp.
475 Park Avenue South
New York, NY 10016

First printing: August, 1987

Printed in the United States of America

PART ONE

1

Sometimes when the wind blew and the long shadows appeared, Long Henry Banner let his thoughts turn inward, bringing him back to when he'd been a captain of infantry with Pickett's Virginians, back to those three days of horror at Gettysburg. Lee had ordered Pickett's division to spearhead the assault upon Union forces entrenched upon the high ground, a *pont au feu*. And so the attack began, and ended that same July afternoon, where thousands on both sides were killed or wounded, and with darkness obscuring the retreat of Lee's defeated forces. Capt. Henry Banner, just turned 22, one of the walking wounded, fought on until Lee surrendered his southern forces at Appomattox. Then he returned to his Virginia home, only to find that his parents were dead, the small farmhouse blackened embers, and shortly thereafter he headed west, vowing never to return to the land of his youth.

Now Long Henry stared westward, past the outer limits of Waco to where campfires flickered near herd grounds. Three months ago he'd been taken on as marshal of this sprawling cattle town, a waystop on the

Chisholm Trail running up from Old Mexico to the railhead at Abilene, Kansas. It was just another job, a place which would probably hold him for a spell before the wanderlust took hold again. He heard the sound of hoofs, and then by moonlight several riders bobbed under wide-brimmed hats, and for the briefest of moments the notion struck him that some pickets were heading in through the lines, but the war between the states had ended nine years ago. In passing, one of the cowhands struck light to a cigarette, while the other riders glanced casually at Long Henry watching their silent passage. Young and feisty, thought Long Henry. Probably didn't have one double eagle amongst the lot of them, not until they delivered their herd to the buyers at Abilene. They'd do some drinking, raise a little hell, then on the brightening side of midnight head back to their herd.

"Better make my rounds," Long Henry murmured silently, moving back toward main street along the dusty backtrail left by the horses.

On main street, he stepped under a stretch of covered boardwalk, while street lamps revealed the timbered walls and roofs of new buildings under construction. During the past two years Waco had almost doubled in size. Mule trains brought in lumber and most of the necessities of life, and on the stagecoaches came those seeking a new life, some honest folks, but mostly tinhorns, outlaws or fancy ladies. And also to Waco came the cattle buyers, cattle barons, the moneylenders. By Long Henry's estimate there were five trail herds bedded down on the plains to the southwest; about the average number that passed through every week during these torrid summer months.

He came to a cross street and drew up, and as his habit was; Long Henry gauged the night sounds borne to him by the sultry wind moving disdainfully along the wide and dusty thoroughfare—raucous laughter, piano music floating out of a saloon across the street, the clatter of hoofs drumming on the street hardened to iron by a scarcity of rain, and the distant lowing of cattle. The yellowed and wavering light above revealed the watchful gleam in Long Henry's brown eyes, and too, the sense of isolation there, but from under the brim of the Stetson they were constantly checking off every item in view, missing nothing. He was a tall and rock-lean southerner, clean-shaven, and with ruggedly handsome features. There were others here of an equal height, but Long Henry seemed to stand taller than these men. Maybe it was because of his erect carriage, or the way he moved and talked that made others give him a second look in passing. His clothes were neat but trailworn, and hanging at his right hip was a .45 Colt Dragoon.

Ahead and on the same side of the street a cowhand spun outside through batwing doors and staggered off the boardwalk to the street. Another hand emerged from the saloon and said sharply to the one in the street, "Let it lay, Curly! That gambler was dealing square!"

"He's a damn sidewinder that needs killing!"

"Curly, you're three sheets under." The hand stepped down into the street to his companion, who tore away from the restraining hand, moved onto the boardwalk and back through the batwings.

Long Henry shoved inside through the swinging

9

batwings, quickly sized up the situation, the drunken cowhand heading for a back table, where everyone rose to move out of the way except for the man sitting with his back to the wall, smoke from the Mex cigarette curling up past the watchful eyes.

"Tinhorn!" the hand blurted out, wiping his right hand on his leather chaps, "Ain't nobody in Texas that lucky at faro!"

"Two things I hate," the gambler said calmly, "drunks and sore losers." He gestured with his left hand at the pile of chips there. "How much you figure you're out?"

"Damn you, tinhorn, Curly Moore don't take charity from no double-dealer!"

The gambler, a man of indeterminate age, sighed wearily, his eyes flicking past the hand to the marshal of Waco closing on the table. Carefully he reached up and touched his expansive mustache which was tinged with gray while the ghost of a smile touched his wide mouth. His shaggy hair below the flat-crowned hat was gray-speckled, the face narrow and swarthy, and the gambler wore a black frock coat and dark red vest.

Close now, Long Henry could see the muscles in the cowhand's shoulder bunching to go into action and the fingers of the right hand curling nervously just above the holstered gun. Movement up by the bar ceased, with the tinkling notes of the piano ceasing in mid-song as the piano player eased off the stool, while those who'd been talking fell silent. And then the hand made his play, reaching clumsily for the butt of his holstered gun, only to have Long Henry knock the weapon away, and with his own gun Long Henry clubbed the hand at the base of the skull. As the hand crumbled at his feet, Long Henry turned his attention to the

10

gambler.

"Much obliged."

"Your handle?"

"Deacon O'Shay."

"You're Mexican, aren't you?" he asked, and wondering why the gambler wasn't with his own kind at the cantinas located on the southern fringes of town.

The gambler shrugged. "My father was Irish. And I don't make it a practice of short-dealing cowboys. Especially Texans. Because they've got short fuses and long memories." Coming to his feet, he slid some chips across the table. "About what he lost, I reckon . . . and a couple more to make him forget that rap to the head." A quick smile revealed even rows of teeth.

"Maybe," drawled Long Henry, and smiled back. Holstering his gun, he turned around and spoke to the other hand. "Get your pard back to your herd or he'll sleep it off in my jail." He glanced back at the gambler. "Figure on being in town long?"

"Could be—"

"Just don't overstay your welcome."

"Never do, Marshal Banner."

Long Henry continued on his rounds, which included Waco's many gambling houses, variety theaters and dance halls. It was closing on midnight by the time he returned to the jail to tell the deputy there that he was calling it a night. Angling across the street, he entered the lobby of the Frontier Hotel, an imposing three-storied structure, and with a lighted arcade running along its facade. From force of habit he studied those people in the lobby, by their clothing some cattle buyers and ranchers, and an immigrant family of five clustered around an overstuffed divan behind which on

11

the wall there was a large framed painting showing some Pawnee Indians attacking a stagecoach. He found himself staring at the young woman, and a feeling of restlessness stirred in Long Henry, and of longing. All he'd done since coming west was find an odd job, cowboying, prospecting, then drift again when the urge came to him. He was tired of being a loner, realized that sooner or later he must put down roots someplace, with a woman like this filling the void in his heart.

"Just a dream," he murmured bitterly to himself, and heading for the circular staircase.

"Evening, Henry."

He glanced that way to see Doc Sam Holter emerging from the dining room corridor. "Smoking imported cigars again. Guess your patients are paying you in cash money now."

"Yup, it sure does make for better relationships." Doc Holter had a full head of white hair; a few strands curled over his coat collar. In his mid-fifties, he was lean, and wearing a light summer suit and a look of concern. "Look like you had a bad day?"

"The heat, I reckon."

Upstairs in his room, Long Henry dropped his hat on the dresser and moved through the darkness to a window and gazed past the serrated buildings opposite to where heat lightning flared along the distant horizon. Again thoughts of the war, and of battles fought, of comrades long dead, paraded through his mind. They'd fought the good fight, but it was over, long over. Reflecting on it now, he realized he had little rancor for the North, that coming out here had turned him into a westerner. Marshalling was a dangerous

12

business though, so maybe he'd better forget about settling down with a good woman. Suddenly the night closed in upon him, and over the marshal of Waco came a great weariness. Undressing, he sought the iron-framed bed and the release which sleep would bring. But sleep came hard. And then only after the young immigrant woman Long Henry had seen in the lobby had struck west out of Waco and his dream-clutched thoughts.

2

Casandra Ashbury had no regrets about the life she'd led, nor would she regret leaving New Orleans. She'd even enjoyed working at the Plantation House, one of the city's more reputable whorehouses. More than one southern gentleman had wanted her to become his mistress. But Casandra wanted far more than that, and for this reason she had decided to strike out west.

This decision had been reached only after Navajo Killane had come in one night, and after gazing into his lazy green cat eyes she knew they'd become lovers. He was unlike any man she'd ever known before, savage in his lovemaking, hardbodied, and always aware of everything that was going on around him. Without asking, Casandra knew that he'd killed some men. The other girls there were afraid of him, while Madame Boviar's mulatto gave Killane a wide berth. This physical attraction they had for one another, she mused, could destroy her, for Navajo Killane was not the man she wanted to marry.

Long ago in West Virginia when she was growing up, the only child of an uneducated wildcatter, Casandra had vowed that someday she'd be wealthy. The day after her sixteenth birthday she ran away, securing passage on a southbound train. Her first lover, a carpetbagger, had plucked her off the train and into a Savannah hotel. In the weeks and months to come there were a succession of other men and towns. And she discarded these men as she'd discarded her last name, and when Casandra Ashbury arrived in New Orleans, a few inquiries led her to the Plantation House, where she was immediately hired by its proprietor, an aging Frenchwoman named Madame Boviar.

Now Casandra framed a smile for the plump middle-aged man donning his clothes. In a soft caressing drawl she said, "That was just marvelous, Mr. Milburn."

"Cassie," he said, and sliding some money under one of the pillows on the bed, "you bring out the best in me." He cast a passionate glance at the lissome body enclosed in the red chemise.

And beyond him she gazed at her reflection showing in the floor length mirror. Her creamy skin was flawless, with the tresses of flowing raven hair falling to a tiny waist. She had full breasts and long legs, and high cheekbones below wide violet eyes, eyes that were rimmed with mascara and could sweep a man into their fathomless depths or cast him away with a look of withering scorn. To Casandra Ashbury her beauty was a weapon she was fully determined to use to get what she wanted out of life. The man in her bedroom meant nothing to her, nor did any of her other customers, but Navajo Killane had struck in her a responsive chord, for they, she had instantly realized, were of the same hard breed, would kill if anyone got in their way. She didn't love Killane. Nor did he love her, she sensed. But they needed one another. And in order to survive, she would have to dominate that relationship. For Killane had no other ambitions than gambling and women. As she moved toward the bedroom door, the man reached for her arm and drew her close.

"You know, my dear, I just might decide to stay all night."

"Mr. Milburn," she murmured, "you know the house rules." She guided him to the door, which she opened and stepped ahead of him out into the hallway. The smile went away when she saw Madame Boviar and her mulatto servant standing at the head of the staircase.

"Glad to have had you with us, Mr. Milburn," gushed Madame Boviar, a fleshy woman with washed-out brown hair.

"Be here again next week." He handed Madame Boviar some money and went down the stairs.

"You took long enough with him," she hissed.

"If you say so," Casandra said icily.

"Don't you get uppity with me, whore! I've a good mind to let Sam here work you over again. And I don't want to see that damned breed Killane here no more. You hear, girl?"

"He left town," she replied.

"About time. Well, don't just stand there. You've got another customer waiting downstairs."

Wordlessly, Casandra started down the stairs, the anger in her carefully under control. Tonight Navajo Killane would come for her. She'd packed what possessions she owned in a saddlebag. However, they were desperately in need of a grubstake, and the cold

16

glimmer in Casandra Ashbury's eyes came from the thought that before leaving here tonight she intended to rob Madame Boviar.

Around four o'clock the large house had quieted down, and Casandra Ashbury, dressed in riding clothes, removed the revolver Navajo Killane had given her from an empty saddlebag. She'd gotten used to the feel of the weapon, having gone with Killane outside the city for some target practice. Picking up the saddlebag containing her clothes, she turned out the gas lamp, opened the latticed door and eased out onto the balcony running around the second floor. Carefully she crept to where the balcony overlooked the alley, and dimly she could make out Killane seated in the saddle. She tossed down the saddlebag, which he caught and placed behind the saddle of the other horse. When he looked up again Casandra had vanished.

On the second floor hallway, holding the other saddlebag and the revolver, Casandra paused when she reached the landing and sharpened her ears to the night sounds coming from inside the house, those filtering in from the city. Down the hallway, the faint creak of bed springs came from one of the rooms, and she knew that Madame Boviar had let a customer stay overnight with one of the girls. And about this time every night Madame Boviar would be in her small cubicle of an office counting the day's take, while the mulatto, Sam, would be asleep in the adjoining bedroom. She'd talked Killane out of taking a part in this, remembering the beating given to her by the mulatto, and though Casandra hadn't killed before, a part of her wanted to do just that to the mulatto if he interfered. Now she slipped down the staircase.

She took the dark hallway to the left, grateful for the thick carpeting, and remembered as she came to the office door to cock the revolver. Then Casandra stiffened in alarm when she heard the sound of voices coming from behind the door. The mulatto was there. But an icy calm settled over her as she turned the knob and swung the door ajar.

"Don't try it!" Casandra lashed out, as the mulatto started to shove up from the chair, while the woman gaped in surprise from where she sat at the table, the day's receipts spread out before her.

"What is this?" snapped Madame Boviar.

"I want that money on the table! And what you've got in the safe too!"

"You're crazy! Get her, Sam!"

Smiling craftily, the mulatto eased upward. He was large, thick through the shoulders, and with long, powerful arms. No fear showed in his black eyes, only a mocking confidence. He said gruffly, "The only weapon you like, hussy, is what a man's got between his legs." He held out a hand for the weapon while shuffling toward Casandra.

Pow!

The bullet caught the mulatto in the chest. He stopped and staggered slightly, the full mouth of white teeth showing in an angry snarl, and came at her again. Two more times the gun sounded, the second slug piercing the man's right eye, and his lifeless body crumpled to the floor at Casandra's feet. Quickly she sprang forward to drop the saddlebag on the table.

"The money, you old witch!"

Somehow a frightened Madame Boviar managed to

18

shove the money into the saddlebag, and then Casandra lashed out again. "Now the safe!"

"No . . . you . . . you'll clean me out . . ."

Coming around the table, she slapped the woman across the face, then shoved Madame Boviar toward the safe. "I want all of it!"

The fight seemed to go out of Madame Boviar, and fighting back the tears, she turned away and slid a hand inside the safe, but now a gleam of triumph flashed in her eyes because the hand that emerged from the safe held a small derringer. "Here . . . here's the money," she muttered, turning around to face Casandra, but before she could fire, the gun held by Casandra bucked, and a small moan of pain and shock issued from the older woman's lips when the slug found her stomach, the reflex action of her trigger finger firing a bullet from the derringer which scoured a path across the top of the table. Then her lifeless eyes followed the flight of her body toward the floor.

Casandra's knees buckled and some of the color drained from her face as she realized that she'd just killed two people. But she fought back the brief moment of weakness when she heard the sound of voices coming from the upper floor. Quickly she removed all of the money from the safe, shoved it into the saddlebag and hurried out into the hallway, to move along its dark length until she found a side door which took her out into the alley where Navajo Killane was waiting.

"What happened?"

She scrambled into the saddle and placed the saddlebag over the shoulders of her horse before taking the reins from Killane, and without uttering a word, urged her horse deeper into the alley at a lope and out onto the next street, with Killane bringing up the rear. At a gallop they went through the French Quarter to find their way to the waterfront and northward along the Mississippi River. But before they were clear of the outer fringes of the city, Killane reached for the reins of her horse and brought both mounts to a prancing halt.

"I asked you what happened?"

They'd stopped under light cast by a street lamp, and her cold eyes swept over his dark, hawkish face. Calmly she said: "I killed the mulatto . . . and the old bitch . . ."

His hard eyes studied her face, then Navajo Killane's thin lips parted to reveal gold teeth shining in a gold-glittering smile. "Beauty is only skin deep, Cassie gal." The gentle breeze rippled against Killane's long shaggy black hair, and he wore the gear of a working cowhand.

"What's that supposed to mean?"

"It means that some day you might do the same to me for the gold . . . in these teeth."

Her anger was blunted by the smile, and she said, "Let's just forget what happened tonight."

"I just hope the New Orleans police will do the same," he said, as they set out at a slower pace. Within a few moments they were swallowed up by the night.

Dawn found them crossing over to the western side of the Mississippi on a small barge, and then they headed to the southwest for most of the morning. A small town appeared ahead of them; Belle Chasse. Now Casandra felt tired, drained by what had happened last night, but no flicker of conscience stirred within her. She had just surmounted another obstacle on her way to a better life. It had been agreed that they'd split up at Belle Chasse, Killane to head to Shreveport, and she would take the train into Texas and up to Waco. She'd miss what Killane had given her, more than she cared to admit to herself, and after they'd ridden into Belle Chase and found a room at a small inn, their need for one another brought them into the bed and each other's seeking arms.

3

Long Henry rose at dawn and went for a ride along the Brazos River, letting the grulla set its own meandering pace. The stubbles of grass were heavy with dew, and though mist still hung low over the river, the heat of day was beginning to build.

He enjoyed these moments of solitude. At times like these he could even forget that he'd fought for a losing cause, even think about buying some land and starting a ranch. He smiled at a mule deer emerging from the brush and easing down onto the red-loamy bank. The grulla nickered, and the deer gazed that way for a long searching moment before bolting away.

Texans, he'd found out, were a close-mouthed bunch, knowing who their neighbors were but not interfering too much, and lending a helping hand without waiting to be asked. But to Waco had come a new breed. Merchants and carpetbaggers from back east; most of them not giving a damn about those southerners who'd moved out here too. Such a man was Jed Bullock, a johnny-come-lately with a sizable bankroll. Bullock's general store had branched out into other lines — real estate and the cattle game. And as a member of Waco's town council Jed Bullock had been dead set against the hiring of a former Reb officer to the position of marshal.

Every day saw more of the rough element coming to Waco. Sooner or later, Long Henry realized, he or one of his deputies would be involved in a gunfight, and to counteract this, he'd suggested to the town council that all newcomers leave their weapons at the jail. Jed Bullock had been vehemently opposed to this ordinance, had barely stopped short of calling the marshal of Waco a coward. The council would meet at mid-morning to vote on Long Henry's proposal.

Out on the brackish waters a fish jumped, and was gone in about the time it would take a man to blink. Long Henry stared at the concentric rings rippling into ever-widening circles, and squinted beyond the river to where sunlight was beginning to filter through motionless cottonwoods, then he urged his horse up a break in the bank and onto the undulating plains stretching west of Waco.

He found some high ground and studied the movements of the herds. Distantly he could see a couple of herds strung out north of Waco. Visible southward was another column of dust, and he knew that before this day had run its course at least two or three more herds would arrive, and with the cowhands coming into town. He thought about the incident last night involving that gambler, Deacon O'Shay, and the cowpuncher. Though O'Shay had given the appearance of a man who would give a man a fair shake, there were plenty of others here who wouldn't have thought twice about gunning down a drunken hand. And Long

Henry was worried about some of his younger deputies, knowing that in a town like Waco a man's first mistake was generally his last. But at least they knew what they were getting paid to do, to uphold law and order and maybe die for it too.

"What are you getting paid for?" Long Henry asked himself. During the war it was the Cause, which wasn't the question of slavery as most thought, but of the right of every southern state to be free of a central tyranny, the federal government at Washington. He was sixteen when the war started, and his parents wouldn't give him permission to enlist. Many a lonely day would find him slipping off to a secluded glade on the farm where he'd do his youthful dreaming, and where the softest of winds rippled through rich green grass and across the millpond carrying with it the scent of honeysuckle and fresh clover. Above the rustling foliage the heroes of his youth would ride across the gray-speckled sky; Jackson, Longstreet, Lee, as would a young woman beckoning to him from the western horizon, and though in his dreams he tried to catch her, sundown would always find her slipping away. Of those southern generals only the brooding and black-bearded James Longstreet was still alive, and Long Henry Banner hadn't dreamed about that young woman since he'd left Virginia. Glory, Honor, the Cause; the hope of all southerners. Out here there were just the plains, the dust, the torrid heat, the law of the gun. And he reckoned he was getting paid to protect the interests of the merchants and the few honest folks in Waco. Maybe he should ride on. But if he did certain men would sully his name.

At the touch of his spurs the grulla swung down the

slope and toward Waco. He came to the stagecoach road, and swinging onto it, pulled out the makings and rolled a cigarette into shape. Strange, he mused, that old memories of home should come back to him now. By his way of thinking he was getting beyond the marriage age. He was cautious, a patient man, but maybe too patient, waiting as he had all these years for the woman of his dreams to come along.

"Hoss," he drawled bitterly, dragging smoke into his lungs, "In Texas sentimentality and memories can get a man a parcel of land in Boot Hill."

The members of the town council quieted down when the mayor of Waco called the meeting to order, but from the comments that had filtered to him where he sat off by himself in a hard-backed chair, Marshal Banner sensed that matters wouldn't go his way.

"Mayor," spoke up Rubin Corley, the owner of a dry goods store, "water is shore getting scarce. We need another well."

"We ain't meetin' this morning, Corley, to talk about water. Which is somethin', I noticed, you shy away from drinkin'." Mayor Art Lindley stroked his wide mustache, and he had a habit of breathing audibly through his mouth. His hair was streaked with gray and the long sideburns grew over hollowed cheekbones. He gazed past those seated with him around the table and over at the marshal of Waco. "Marshal, supposin' you tell us more about this no gun-toting proposal—"

"I say the marshal's proposed ordinance is unconstitutional."

The mayor glared at city attorney Matt Simmons, a dapper man with a lean face and cynical eyes. "According to some of your political speeches, Matt, so are the ten commandments." Lindley stroked his mustache. "You've got the floor, Banner."

Rising, Long Henry placed his hat on the chair and ambled over to the table. He sought the eyes of the eight men seated there, only to have most of them look elsewhere. He knew them only as merchants, the men who'd hired him, and if he was gunned down while serving as their marshal, the knowledge was plain to him that most of these men wouldn't come to his funeral, the cost of it coming out of his wages. They were transplanted easterners, the new breed of mercenaries, men who wanted so desperately to be called Texans, but would raise a ruckus if a cowhand came calling on one of their daughters.

He found himself gazing at Jed Bullock. On his rounds, he had seldom seen Bullock's wife venturing out onto the streets, but more than once he'd caught a glimpse of Bullock heading out to the Mex cribs south of town. He'd kept this knowledge to himself, as he had about the various habits of the other men here; that was something that went with the job, he reckoned. Jed Bullock seemed cut from a different bolt of cloth than the others, the cold glimmer in his eyes one of mocking surety, a hard man who, Long Henry recalled, had taken court action against those who couldn't pay off their bills, and Bullock would use his position on the town council to further his own ambitions.

"I know how most of you feel about being heeled," Long Henry began cautiously, "that you feel naked without a gun handy." He saw the swell of self-importance on some of their faces, knowing that the majority here didn't know the difference between a twelve-gauge and a pump-action carbine. "But things are changing. Waco is growing into something bigger than a large town. Soon it'll be a city. But in order to control a larger populace you need a gun ordinance. Mr. Plummer, as a banker, I know you'd feel a lot safer if there were fewer guns around."

"Marshal," cut in Jed Bullock, "we get a lot of needed revenue from the cattlemen. We take the guns away from their hands when they hit town, why, it'll be no time a'tall before the trail herds stop coming here. Now, Banner, if you don't feel up to the job, just say so . . ."

Though Long Henry could feel his temper rising, he said calmly, "When a drunken hand . . . or an outlaw goes for his weapon . . . he doesn't care who he kills. One of these times it could be one of you . . . or your wife or child. And believe me, gentlemen, it'll happen."

"Come now, Banner," spoke up another member of the council, "this is the west. And I like things the way they are. Anyway, we're paying you to keep law and order. Sorry, Marshal, but I'm going to side with Jed Bullock on this."

"Let them keep their weapons."

"We need the business."

"Yes, yes, no sense taking any chances . . . that the trail bosses won't have their herds stop here."

"Order!" said the mayor. "Now, those in favor of the marshal's proposal will raise their hands."

The hesitant hand of the banker went up, and the mayor voted for Long Henry's proposed ordinance, and with a quiet nod the marshal of Waco retrieved his hat and left the town hall building. He would have to live with the council's decision. But when word got out that Waco was a town that was ruled by the gun, more and more tinhorns would push in. At least he understood that money was the divining rod by which this town lived, survived. The heat hammered at Long Henry as he moved along the boardwalk, and glancing into a window of the dry goods store, saw that the hands on the wall clock were set at half past eleven, though the position of the sun also told him that. The hot sultry air seemed to be filled with a static electricity. When was the last time it had rained? A month ago; June. But just enough to fill in the parched cracks on the streets and freshen the air. Now with summer about at full strength, the temperature pushing over the hundred mark, the townspeople were on edge. The need for a beer, to still the thirst in him, and also to cool down his displeasure at what had just happened, drew him into the Antler Saloon, where he found one of his deputies, Tilwell, standing alone at the back end of the bar.

"How'd it go?"

"Bill, they voted against it." He motioned for the barkeep to refill Tilwell's beer stein, and that he wanted one for himself.

"Thanks to Bullock," Tilwell muttered bitterly. "Some mighty rough hombres are in town. Not that I'm going to back down from them. But it would set better in my mind if they weren't heeled."

After Long Henry had emptied the stein of beer, he waved away Tilwell's offer to buy him a second, then went outside and across the street toward the Wells

Fargo office. His mail usually contained one or two reward posters, but his real purpose for watching the arrival of the noon stage was to make a mental note of the passengers. About a half dozen people were clustered under the covered boardwalk, and he stepped there to stand beside the Wells Fargo agent.

The agent said sourly: "This heat's intolerable. Intolerable." With a blue-checkered handkerchief he wiped his perspiring forehead. Strands of hair were combed across the crown of his head to hide the bald spot. His movements were listless; those of a man approaching his sixties, and sapped by the heat too.

"Bad day for traveling," agreed Long Henry. "Will the stage be on time?"

"Expect so."

Nearly fifteen minutes passed before a plume of dust appeared to the east. Then the stagecoach could be seen ahead of the dust, distorted by the shimmering heat waves. More people emerged from buildings, as did members of the town council, some of whom crossed over to station themselves along the boardwalk.

When the driver reined up the sweat-lathered horses in front of the Wells Fargo building, some of those watching surged forward, not really expecting to meet anyone they knew, just merely a way of breaking up daily routine. The man riding shotgun, Jack Dunn, a former army scout, Long Henry recalled, clambered from his seat to the top of the coach and began untying the luggage piled there, while the agent opened the passenger door, stepped aside to wipe his brow again. The first passenger to emerge was a drummer, then a couple of hardcases who quickly moved away from the scrutinizing gaze of the marshal, went down the street and turned the corner. As the luggage was handed down to the agent, a young woman appeared in the open door of the coach, and the eyes of every man there went to her as she placed a trim foot on the support step. She paused to slowly let her steady and bold eyes sweep the faces of the bystanders, discarding each man until they lighted on Long Henry, where they held, with an inviting smile parting her full lips.

Long Henry felt something stirring within him. As he stared back at the woman the sounds of Waco seemed to fade away. Now he thought of another woman he'd known back in Virginia, a girl really, whom he'd worshipped from afar until she up and married the son of a plantation owner. But that girl had never been the woman of his dreams. Only when the woman tore her eyes away and smiled at the man who had just stepped to her and held out a supporting arm, did it occur to Long Henry that she was an enchantress, the most beautiful woman he had ever seen. A dark-haired and willowy beauty. Then he felt a stab of resentment when he suddenly realized that it was Jed Bullock who had helped the woman dismount from the stagecoach, and who had claimed the woman's luggage. Bullock; ever the opportunist. The man certainly looked the part of the successful businessman with his black suit and string tie, the head of wavy brown hair, but the gleam in the man's eyes, Long Henry had noticed, was possessive, lust-filled.

Long Henry went into the Wells Fargo office, thinking that it was foolish to get riled up over a smile from a woman he'd never met, and besides, from the cut of the woman's clothes, there was little he could offer her.

His possibles consisted of a warbag, saddle and horse. Still, he had seen that smile in the sky of his dreams, the feeling coming to him that she just could figure in his future plans.

4

The only difference between New Orleans and this rawboned western town, Casandra Ashbury had found out a week later, was the scarcity of women, with the few she'd seen on the streets wearing long gingham dresses, though those working at the dance halls and saloons were clothed more garishly. The men were the same—lusty, wanting a good time, and willing to pay for it. But here she was seeking a different life than the one she'd led back in New Orleans.

Only after Navajo Killane had seen her aboard a westbound train and it was well on its way toward Texas, did Casandra discover that Killane had taken most of the money she'd stolen from Madame Boviar. Her first angry thought had been to go after him. But even if she found him, Killane would have probably lost the money at the gambling tables. So at Texarkana she'd got on the stage that brought her here to Waco, and after paying for a month's lodging, she was down to her last forty dollars.

Her daily forays from her suite in the Frontier Hotel found Casandra eating alone in the restaurant at the hotel or venturing along the bustling streets wearing the clothing of a grieving southern widow. She'd let it be known that her husband had died late last year, and wanting a change of scenery, had sold their Savannah plantation and come out here.

Casandra had been coolly polite to the men she'd met, and had only caught an occasional glimpse of the marshal of Waco; from one of the hotel clerks she'd been told that Henry Banner wasn't married. And though the first man she'd met here, Jed Bullock, had asked her to go out, she had refused, because Casandra's first impression of Bullock — that he was a vain and shallow man — hadn't changed. But men like Bullock could be twisted around her pretty little finger, would obey her whims with the docility of a plantation slave. This was the power Casandra Ashbury's beauty had given her, and a vision of a world of dazzling wealth.

A cattleman came toward her along the boardwalk, then they both veered toward the front door of Bullock's General Store, with the man tipping his wide-brimmed hat as he opened the door for Casandra. She thanked him with an appreciative smile and went inside. As one of Bullock's clerks waited on the rancher, Casandra went down an aisle to a counter and picked up a lacy scarf, which she held against the bodice of her dark blue dress, and placing it back on the counter, went on to a table laden with bolts of brightly-colored cloth. Then she was aware of Jed Bullock coming out of a back room and hurrying her way.

"Nice to see you again, Mrs. Ashbury." Bullock's bold eyes played over her face.

"This is fine material."

"Here," he said, as he picked out a bolt and unrolled a couple of yards of light blue material, "just the color to match your eyes."

"Yes, it is lovely. Mr. Bullock . . ."

"I'd wish you'd call me Jed—"

"My friends call me Cassie." She smiled into his eyes. "They told me at the hotel you're in the real estate business . . . Jed."

"Some," he admitted.

"My dear, late husband left me some money. Enough to start a small business; perhaps a dress salon."

"Just what this town needs," he agreed. "I know of several places for sale."

"And I would need someone to supply me with material—"

"I'd consider it an honor if you'd open an account here."

"Why, Mr. Bullock, how sweet of you to suggest that." This was the reason Casandra had come to see Bullock. But she had no intention of opening any kind of business, in Waco or any other place. However, because of her lack of funds, and in order to play the role of a wealthy widow, she would need the proper clothes, time to set her plan into operation. Men such as Bullock, she knew, would give her that time. By now a warrant would have been issued for her arrest. But it was the kind of murder that would soon be forgotten by the New Orleans police, because violence and death were nightly occurrences in the city's French Quarter. Madame Boviar, the mulatto: somehow the fact that she'd killed them didn't bother her now. For Casandra had the ability to completely forget about the past.

Some, preachers and the like, would call this a lack of conscience. To Casandra their deaths were merely stepping stones to a grander life. And then there was Navajo Killane; part of her past, and future.

"Do you have any plans for this evening?" he asked anxiously.

"No, Jed, I haven't."

He touched her lightly on the arm, murmured, "An opera singer from the east is performing at the Mystic Theater."

"Are you asking me to go?" she said, and sensing with a woman's intuition that Bullock was a married man. And even if he was, it was of little consequence. To be seen with Bullock, though she still distrusted him, would gain her access to others in the business community.

"We could have supper first at the Frontier Hotel."

"Jed, I'd be delighted to go out with you."

"Splendid," he gushed, and glanced around to see if his clerks were listening to the conversation. "I'll see you around six. Now, Cassie, let's open an account. An open account, I might add."

"Really, Jed, you Texans are so hospitable."

A silence fell upon those dining in the restaurant at the Frontier Hotel when Casandra Ashbury made her appearance. She paused in the wide and open entryway. Her silky raven hair was piled in curls atop her head; the low-bosomed dress emphasized the tiny waist and full hips, and spilling carelessly over her creamy shoulders was a light summer stole. The smile touching her dark ruby lips widened when she spotted Jed

35

Bullock seated alone at a table placed in front of one of the large windows overlooking main street. Discreetly, she'd found out that Bullock was indeed married. A bold, somewhat handsome man, one who made his own rules, she was realizing. Then she swept forward.

The main course had been saddle of veal with dressing, a meal which had been equal to any she'd had in New Orleans, and followed by French coffee and green apple pie. Their conversation had been light, and though Bullock had asked her a few probing questions about her past, these Casandra had parried with a practiced ease. And when Bullock had started to tell her in a boastful way about his plans to expand his business, she saw him more clearly as a man without scruples, certainly not the man who would give her that life of wealth she'd always dreamed about. As he reached across the linen tablecloth to place his hand over hers, she saw the marshal of Waco coming into the dining room, and for some unexplained reason she pulled her hand away.

"Did I offend you, Cassie?"

Quickly she looked back at Bullock. "No . . . it's just that . . . I hardly know you . . . Jed."

A waitress appeared bearing a box of imported Havana cigars, Bullock selected one, lit it and exhaled expansively. He smiled wickedly. "Cassie, tonight I'm the envy of every man in Waco. I hardly need to tell you that you look stunning. Perhaps too stunning for these western women you'll meet tonight."

"Why, Jed, I had no idea. I could go change—"

"You'll do no such thing! These women see what the right clothes can do for them, why, that dress salon of yours will do a land-rush business." From his vest pocket he fished out a round, gold watch. "Time to go, my dear."

Moving ahead of Bullock around the crowded tables, Casandra felt Henry Banner's eyes upon her, and glancing that way, noticed the look of displeasure on his face that she would dine with Jed Bullock. Out in the corridor, where she waited for Bullock to pay for their supper, Casandra was pleased at the look she'd seen on Banner's face. Now she knew that the man was taken with her. In a way he reminded her of Navajo Killane, his sure, easy manner was different though, and he would be a gentleman. But between them was a physical attraction, and a sensuous glimmer danced in her eyes, to go away when Jed Bullock reached her side.

"To the opera, Cassie my dear." He reached possessively for her arm.

"It certainly sounds exciting," she said, with the marshal of Waco still clinging to her thoughts.

For Casandra the evening with Jed Bullock passed in a flurry of excitement. She was introduced to many local merchants and the few ranchers in attendance at the theater. Later, at The Plainsman, one of the few respectable saloons in Waco, she found out from a merchant's wife that in mid-October the Western Stockmen's Association would hold their annual meeting here, with cattle barons from most of the western states expected to be in attendance. At this meeting a lot of money exchanged hands, she was told. And out here prices were high, and Casandra realized now that what money she had left wouldn't last until those cattlemen came to town. The answer to her problem was, of course, finding a man who would keep her until then. Once again the image of the marshal of Waco brought a gleam into her eyes.

"You look happy, Cassie."

"Oh, Jed, just daydreaming, I guess."

"Why don't we go to your suite." Now the slur in his voice was more pronounced, and Casandra knew that he'd been drinking before he came to the hotel. Jed Bullock rose and said his goodnights to those around him, and accompanied by Casandra, he moved out into the sultry night.

Once they were in the Frontier Hotel and on the second floor, Casandra unlocked the door to her suite but left the door closed as she turned to Bullock. "Jed, that was a delightful evening."

His eyes narrowed. "Aren't you going to ask me in?"

"I . . . I still keep thinking of my . . . my dearly departed husband. Surely you must understand . . ."

"I guess so," he growled sullenly. Then he slipped an arm around her shoulders and pulled her close. "Dammit, woman, you must know that I'm crazy about you."

"Please, Jed, you're hurting me."

He kissed her roughly, disdainfully, then stepped away. "Reckon I'm likkered up some, Cassie. But I'll be calling again." Briefly, anger uglied his face, and touching a finger to the brim of his hat, Jed Bullock spun away and found the staircase.

In her suite, Casandra locked the door before moving into her bedroom and lighting a lamp. The evening had gone better than she had expected. Tomorrow she would open charge accounts at other stores. Some of the women she'd met had invited her over to their homes, and she found it amusing that these fine, upstanding women would be horrified if they knew that Casandra Ashbury had been a New Orleans woman of pleasure. Undressing, she examined her lissome body in the dresser mirror before turning out the lamp and crawling into bed, there to have that old craving for Navajo Killane keep her awake far into the night.

5

A widow, Long Henry reasoned, could go out with any man of her choosing, but it still troubled him that Mrs. Ashbury would let Jed Bullock be that man. With an irritated hand he shoved the coffee cup away. Of his five deputies, two were on duty, and creeping across the floor in his office at the jail came evening shadows. This morning he'd caught glimpses of Mrs. Ashbury going into some of the stores, and she seemed a less desirable woman now that he'd seen her in Jed Bullock's company. He shrugged, thinking that she probably didn't know he existed, though a woman like her could sure get to a man, make him careless, or miss a meal or two. As marshal here he couldn't afford not to keep his head straight, especially since the town council had voted against his no-gun proposal.

"Bullock!" he muttered bitterly, and reaching for the makings. He rolled a cigarette into shape, struck light to it. In him was the uneasy knowledge that there was trouble ahead. He'd gotten these same feelings of unrest while fighting with the Confederate army, had learned to pay attention to them. It seemed that of late more and more gunhands were coming to town.

Though he was above average with the gun, some of these owlhooters could be faster on the draw. The door opened and Bridger, one of his deputies, sauntered in, wiped his forehead and with the same hand removed his hat and slapped it against his trouser leg to remove the dust. "Feel like I ate a pound of Texas dirt today, marshal."

"How were things down there?"

"The cantinas are quiet. Even the chickens are too sapped by the heat to do much pecking. But once it cools down, things will liven up. By the way, did you get a gander at that new woman in town. Now that Mrs. Ashbury is some filly, yesirree."

Glaring at his deputy as he rose, Long Henry jammed his hat over his head and let the door slam shut behind him. At the corner, he stopped and fastened a tight grin. "No need to have done that," he chided himself silently. But the truth of the matter was that he couldn't stop thinking about Mrs. Ashbury. Maybe the woman had lied, was still married, had three or four young'uns. "Yup, could be."

The lowering sun appeared below the boardwalk, and squinting into its glare, Long Henry moved along main street. The saloons he passed were quiet, and some of the stores were closing. As he crossed the street toward the hotel, Doc Holter shoved up slowly from one of the benches strung along the arcade.

He said, "Marshal, care to shake for a drink?"

"Might's well, Sam." He went ahead through the open door, through the lobby to the hotel barroom, the walls of which were covered with dark-stained wood and where the heads of game animals were hung, while the bar had been imported from St. Louis, a fancy affair of ornately-carved wood, and with a huge, wall-length mirror that rose to the ceiling. They were the only customers. The barkeep detached himself from the deeper shadows and came toward them, swatting at flies with a rolled up magazine and blinking at the few traces of sunlight coming in through a window.

Doc Holter reached for a dice box. He shook the box with his right hand, then let the dice roll out onto the bar top. "Three fives; I'll leave them."

"The usual, Sam?"

"Yup, and make sure the beer is extra cold."

"Four treys, Sam. Horse on you." Long Henry shook again, watched as the five dice spun and settled on the bar. He enjoyed Doc Holter's company. The man never pushed himself on a person, yet he knew what most folks in Waco were doing, and he never gossiped. When somebody got sick, Doc Holter was always there, and if that person couldn't pay, Holter wouldn't make too much fuss about it. Long Henry came up with a pair of sixes, left them, and shook the other dice again to find he had two more sixes. "Four in two, Sam."

"Tough to beat," remarked Doc Holter, as he picked up the stein and drank deeply. "Ahh . . . been craving that all day."

"Same here," agreed Long Henry.

Two shakes of the dice by Doc Holter failed to beat the four sixes left by Long Henry, and he placed two silver dollars on the bar. "That makes you about three up on me."

"Doc, it's all in the wrist." He laughed softly.

"Henry," snorted Doc Holter, "unless the dice are

42

shaved, or otherwise tampered with, there ain't no man alive who can tell how they'll come out of this here leather box. I'll stake my professional reputation on that."

"You speaking from hard experience?"

"Tell you what, I hate eating alone. What say we shake to see who buys supper?"

Nodding that he would, Long Henry said, "How come you never up and got hitched?"

"Was married back east. Some time back now. To one of them society matrons." He ordered a shot of mash whiskey, and when it came, downed the amber contents in the shot glass in a quick swallow. "But when I told her I had a hankering to come out here . . . well, she up and filed for a divorce. Had no family, and reckon I didn't have that abiding love for her as I should. Anyway, Marshal Banner, here you be in the prime of life. And got a full head of hair to boot. I've seen one or two young fillies hereabouts giving you the eye."

"Getting hitched means settling to one place," he said, and reached for the dice box, and after they'd gone through the ritual of shaking the ivory dice, Doc Holter came up losers again.

Then they found the hallway which brought them to the dining room, and with both men hooking their hats on a coat rack and settling across from one another at a round table. Dusk had settled upon the town, and though the heat was still there, it was cooler in the hotel, and with overhead lamps beaming upon the painted walls. Three ranchers came in and found a table, as did a couple, Scandinavians from the look of them, Long Henry figured. Cowhands seemed to give the place a wide berth, preferring instead to eat at a Mex cafe or others strung along main street. As a waitress arrived to take their order, Doc Holter glanced with speculating eyes beyond Long Henry to the dining room entrance.

"Let's see," murmured Doc Holter, "the brisket of beef. And coffee." He looked at Long Henry. "Here's another young woman giving our esteemed marshal the eye."

Glancing over his shoulder, Long Henry saw to his surprise that he was gazing at Mrs. Ashbury, and that she was coming toward his table. Then she stood looking down at him. "Evening, Marshal Banner. And I do believe you're Doctor Holter."

"Yes . . . yes I am."

Shoving his chair away, Long Henry lurched awkwardly to his feet. "I . . . would you care to join us for supper?"

"It would be my pleasure," replied Casandra Ashbury, and she eased onto a chair to the rustle of satin. "Is it always this hot down here in Texas?"

"The longer one stays the hotter it gets," Doc Holter said dryly. "Ashbury? Knew a family of that name from Virginia."

"Please, gentlemen, call me Cassie. And I lived in Georgia; Savannah. But ever since the war things have changed for the worse. Marshal, I hear you're another southerner."

"Once upon a long ago time," said Long Henry. Until this moment he thought that she never knew he even existed, not that he was complaining. Then he found himself returning her smile, while his eyes played over the long-sleeved dress with its low neck-

44

line. Her perfume came to him, a scent of lilacs, and no dream this, of an enchantress he could never find. Throughout the evening he kept stealing glances at Casandra Ashbury, and too, being vaguely aware of Doc Holter's studious appraisal of the woman, which Long Henry simply put down as nothing more than an older man's envy of youth.

"They say the Brazos is simply lovely this time of year; with the leaves turning and all."

"Ah, yes it is. I . . . would you care to go for a buggy ride on Sunday?"

"I'd be delighted, Henry." Casandra laughed throatily, then rose quickly, with the others coming to their feet. "It seems to be cooler out now. A pleasant evening for a walk." She opened her purse, only to have Doc Holter say that he would pay for her meal.

"Cassie," Long Henry said eagerly, and reddening some, "this town gets a little rough at night. I'd sure admire to walk with you."

"And I accept your offer, Marshal Banner."

Then Long Henry threw Doc Holter an embarrassed grin and escorted Casandra Ashbury out of the dining room. After Doc Holter paid for the meals, he returned to the hotel barroom, and over a shot of whiskey, pondered the sudden appearance of Mrs. Ashbury in the dining room. As a medical doctor he was more a practitioner of people than of what generally ailed them. He had this gut feeling about Casandra Ashbury, that beneath all that beauty was a troubled woman, perhaps a devious one, for she reminded him of a certain species of cactus, the night-blooming cereus with its handsome flowers opening their fragrant blooms about midnight, but beware of its spiny stems, and if the marshal of Waco got mixed up with her, he just might feel the sudden sting of her barbed spines. She'd been out with Jed Bullock; the man was married, but perhaps he hadn't told her that. Other women came in on the stage, those who sought employment at the saloons or cribs, so there was nothing out of the ordinary about her coming here.

"A refill," he said sourly.

"Heat getting to you, doc?"

The glare softened to a quick smile, and he said, "It's getting to all of us, I reckon."

6

Long Henry halted the matched team of bays on a low bluff overlooking the Brazos River. It was warm, windless, a beautiful morning. A few clouds were scattered low to the west, but overhead it was clear, and a huge reddish sun stood low over the bank opposite. The trees spread along the twisting river had hued to gold, brown, red.

In the presence of Casandra Ashbury he felt a sense of contentment, as he had last night when they'd gone for a walk in Waco. Though the invitation had been there, he'd left her at the door to her suite. Now, the touch of her arms on his when he reached up for her was like a simmering branding iron. She loomed above him on the buggy step, the silver cast of the morning light coming through the leafy foliage of the trees outlining her figure, haloing the dark hair brushing against his face, and then her lips were pressing against his, gently, filled with the promise of her. And all of his worries seemed to melt away. At that moment he couldn't plumb the depths of his feelings for Casandra, but under the flannel shirt and leather vest his heart beat harder. One of the horses stepped forward

47

moving the buggy, and only then did Long Henry swing her to the ground, reluctantly let her go.

His face reddened, and he said, "I had no liberties to do that."

"I enjoyed it." Casandra held him with her eyes. Then with a lissome movement she reached for his hand and they turned to study the lay of the river below.

"Not much water left," he commented.

"But the Brazos has a certain elegance, Henry, as you have. And those trees; the color is divine."

During last night's walk he had been more concerned about her presence than by what she'd told him about herself. Today it made little difference. He was contented just to stand here and listen to that melodious southern drawl, to steal glances at the most beautiful woman he'd ever known.

"Over there," she said through a delighted laugh and pointing to a shaded place down close to the river, "would be a marvelous spot to have our lunch. Come." And he responded to the tug of her hand as they turned back to the buggy, where he lifted out a picnic basket.

"I hadn't expected something like this."

"Really, Henry, what's a Sunday ride without a picnic. It's just something I tossed together." Casandra was pleased that the lie came easily from her lips, because the lunch had been prepared by one of the cooks at the hotel. The moment she'd laid eyes upon the marshal of Waco she had selected him as her mark. If she played her cards right this could turn into a deeper relationship, for she knew that one day a reward poster would turn up, and when it did, who would ever suspect Marshal Banner's new bride of being a murderess.

In the days to come Long Henry saw more of Casandra, a few evening walks or buggy rides out onto the plains, or they would dine at the hotel, and once he took her to a variety theater. But it was on one of these evenings in the hotel dining room that Jed Bullock first became aware of the relationship between Casandra and the marshal of Waco.

"Well, Cassie," muttered Bullock, as he paused at their table, "I wasn't aware that you knew our marshal."

"Your marshal is such a charming man, Jed. Would you care to join us?"

"I . . . I'm playing poker tonight." Bullock smiled tightly at Casandra, threw Long Henry a hard glare as he left the dining room.

"The man seems to think he has a claim on you."

"Really, Henry, forget Mr. Bullock. When he asked me to go out I had no idea he was a married man." She reached over and patted his hand.

Nodding, he said, "Are you getting used to our ways?"

"It's all so exciting! Those huge trail herds, the cowhands, and land-sakes, Henry, today I saw one of those mountain men. I hardly think about Savannah anymore."

"Cassie, are you planning on opening a store here?"

"Why do you ask, Henry?"

"One of the merchants happened to mention it."

"Perhaps," she said vaguely. With a flutter of her

hand she brushed a strand of hair away from her face. "Henry, instead of going for a walk, why don't you come up to my suite. Tonight I'm in the mood for talking. You know, you really haven't told me too much about yourself, what you did before you came to Waco. For all I know, Henry, you could be a . . . a bank robber."

They laughed together, a shared moment during which Long Henry gazed deeply into her violet eyes, and suddenly realized that he was very much in love with Casandra Ashbury. The thought unsettled him for a moment, for with this knowledge came the realization that his wandering days were over. He could be chained to a piece of land like any sodbuster or merchant. But to his way of thinking this was that mystery woman of his dreams, and then he found himself leaving the dining room and moving down the corridor to the staircase.

On the second floor, Casandra let them into her suite. When she lighted a lamp, Long Henry saw to his surprise that on a coffee table before a long settee there was a bottle of wine in a metal decanter, and a couple of long-stemmed glasses. He took off his Stetson and held it uncomfortably with both hands, and then Casandra said, "Make yourself at home, Henry, while I go powder my nose." She moved close to him, cupped a hand around his neck and kissed him on the cheek, and throwing him a seductive smile, moved toward her bedroom.

Easing onto the settee, he helped himself to a glass of wine, and after taking a sip, murmured appreciatively, "Not bad."

Out here good women were as scarce as spring

water, and Long Henry knew that he had no right to expect anything from her, but here he was, in the company of the most desirable woman in Waco, or Texas, for that matter. During his growing years he'd been to church some, but when he headed out on his own after the war, working as a cowhand then riding shotgun for Wells Fargo before taking over as sheriff here, he'd explored the sensuous delights of one or two women. Casandra Ashbury was different somehow, the kind you married, tipped your hat to. Though it rankled him, he could see men like Jed Bullock going after someone like Casandra. But after all, he reasoned, he sure hadn't been bashful about his own intentions, though all he'd done was hold her hand or steal a kiss.

"Henry—"

Her throaty voice seemed to come from a great distance, and twisting sideways on the settee, he gazed upon a Casandra Ashbury he'd never seen before. She seemed to glide away from the bedroom door and toward him, the lamplight touching her burnished head of flowing raven hair, while the red silky robe she wore was secured at her waist by a thin belt. Only when she sank down next to him on the settee did he realize the robe was all she had on, that through its shimmering folds he could see the outline of her bosom.

"Casandra," he stammered, "I . . ."

"We'll talk later, darling," she whispered, as her arms encircled his neck. Then, somehow, the robe fell open to expose the nakedness underneath, and when she reached to turn down the flame on the lamp, Long Henry didn't see the cold, calculating gleam in Casandra's eyes.

A week later they were married. Marshal Banner and his bride took up residence in a wood-framed house north of town. He found that he had to pay off Cassandra's lodging bill at the Frontier Hotel, but it was a small price to pay, he figured, to live with the woman he loved. His routine became that of hurrying home at noon, or if the town was quiet, of quitting early. He also found out that his wife hated to be cooped up at home. Generally she'd be uptown shopping, and to his dismay many of the merchants would waylay him when he was making his rounds and ask him to pay something on his wife's accounts. He paid these bills, taking some solace in the sight of Cassandra looking more lovely than ever in the new clothes she'd bought.

7

Autumn had given way to the colder days of October. And now that the northern states were winterbound, the trail herds had stopped coming through Waco. Once in a while a cold rain would lash down upon the town. But toward the end of the month the weather cleared and Waco welcomed members of the Cattlemen's Association, those cattle barons coming here from all of the western states for the association's annual meeting, taking over the Frontier Hotel, spreading out from there to the saloons, gambling houses, variety theaters and dance halls. Cattle buyers came also, and gamblers and gunhands. At the insistence of the town council the meeting would last two weeks.

Long Henry thought about this as he strolled along main street, and wondering if he should hire more deputies. With the presence of these cattlemen the action became wild and woolly, and once they got liquored up, there could be some gunplay. Last week, he'd mentioned this to one of the members of the town council, Jed Bullock, and had been told by Bullock that if he couldn't handle matters with the deputies he had, that he should up and quit. And it seemed strange to him that a married man such as Bullock should be bitterly resentful over his marriage to Casandra. It could be that the man was still taken with Casandra, but as long as Bullock kept his distance, Long Henry would keep his notions on the matter to himself.

Saddle horses were tied at every saloon fronting main street, and on side streets also, along with a few buggies, and people crowded the boardwalks. Earlier this afternoon he'd stopped at his house expecting to find Casandra, but she hadn't been there, and now he paused in front of the Roundup Saloon and gave the street a cursory look in the hopes of spotting her.

"Must be shopping again," he said, and went inside. A few muleskinners were piking at a monte game, three card tables were in operation, mostly by townspeople, and then he was easing up to where Doc Holter stood at the crowded bar.

"Doc, how goes it?"

"Tolerable."

"I haven't seen you around much lately."

"Been busy, Henry," he said quietly.

"By the way, have you seen Cassie?"

"Nope," Doc Holter replied. He had in fact seen Casandra going into the Frontier Hotel about an hour ago. And strolling by on the boardwalk had glanced in through a dining room window to catch a glimpse of her sitting at a table with an older man, a rancher, he had thought at the time. He felt that it wasn't up to him to keep tabs on any man's wife. The woman was a temptress, he sensed, playing some kind of con game, and to his way of thinking it was too bad that she'd involved Henry Banner in it. According to the Good Book, however, a man had to honor the marriage of a friend, and the marshal was just that, a young man with a tough job and a beautiful wife who seemed to enjoy the attentions of other men. Yup, that cactus flower was blooming, and the sun was still high in the sky.

The owner of the saloon, Matt Bascomb, a burly man with a receding hairline, and a nose too long for his pitted face, set a stein of beer before Long Henry, then wiped some spillage from the nicked bar top with a grimy rag. "Marshal," he said with some concern and a little quieter than was his habit, "you ever hear of a gunslinger name of Navajo Killane?"

"Killane?" Long Henry sipped at his beer.

"I have," ventured Doc Holter. "Operates out of Arizona, New Mexico. Got eleven notches on his gun, I've heard."

"Yeah, Doc Holter's right; Killane comes from over New Mexico way."

"So, what about this Killane?"

Bascomb nodded over at one of the tables. "Got some of the locals in a high stakes game. No need for me to point him out."

Casually, the marshal of Waco wedged a boot on the railing and turned sideways to look at the card table. It was Killane's eyes that held him first, the bright greenness of them, and contrasting vividly with the savage Indian features and mane of shaggy black hair falling to the sloped shoulders. There seemed to be no spark of life, no emotion, in those eyes as Navajo Killane went about the business of playing poker, and the other players were quiet too, but tensed up somehow, as if they knew the inevitable outcome of the game, and were afraid to cash in what chips they had left for fear of offending the stranger in their midst. The flat-crowned black hat was pushed to the back of Killane's head. The fancy black leather vest and shirt covered what upper body Long Henry could see, and the hands that held the cards or reached to throw a chip into the pot were slender with long, tapering fingers. Even though some sunlight seeped in through the dusty window panes, inside the saloon it was murky, the unpainted walls and low ceiling adding to this darkness, and then what happened next caused a stir of unease in Long Henry, because Navajo Killane suddenly smiled as he raked in another pot to reveal gold-studded teeth, that through some mystical means caught what light there was and sparkled. And now the gunslinger laughed, a sound as of a cold wind slithering over a tombstone, and Long Henry knew that he was in the presence of evil.

"Taking your wife to the dance tonight?"

He cast Doc Holter a distracted glance. "Cassie insists that we go."

Holter smiled. "Seems the honeymoon is over. Well, I'd best get back to the office. See you around."

After Holter had left, Long Henry turned around and planted his elbows on the bar. On the back bar and up behind the bottles was an old calendar showing all of the months in squared sections and a picture of a moss-backed longhorn surrounded by a pack of timber wolves. Nobody had ever consulted the calendar as far as he knew, but Bascomb liked the picture of the steer, bragging that the moss-back had the situation pretty much under control. The barkeeper could be right,

56

Long Henry mused, but he was having a tough time making ends meet now that most of his monthly salary went toward paying off his wife's creditors. He wanted Cassie to stay home more, the fact that she hadn't been home this afternoon edging into the worry of his thoughts. She'd professed her love for him, and she was passionate enough, then again, could be that he was blinded by her beauty, because there were times when he'd detect a cold glimmer in her eyes, as if she was blocking him and Waco out of her mind. She had a will of her, that was for sure. When he picked up his stein and sipped at the beer it tasted flat, and he put the glass down hard, with some of the beer left slopping out and splashing onto the sleeve of the man standing to his left.

"Watch it!" the man grumbled, and glaring at Long Henry, only to back off when he saw the challenging set to the marshal's face, and then Long Henry left the saloon.

Back at the jail, Long Henry searched through the reward posters to see if there was one on Navajo Killane. Then he opened those which had come in with the day's mail. "Nothing," he murmured, and reminding himself to tell his deputies to keep an eye on the gunslinger.

The only other piece of mail was an official-looking letter from the territorial judge down in Austin, and opening it, he found out that he was expected to be there on Friday to testify at the trial of a cattle rustler. Grimacing, he crumbled up the letter and tossed it into a trash basket. He'd have to catch Wednesday's stage; Sunday was the earliest he could get back here. A bad time for this to come up. For the next couple of weeks this would be a wide-open town, a no-holds-barred celebration wanted by the town council. Some of his deputies were inexperienced, and if someone got shot, could they handle the situation? As for Cassie, all she had talked about for the past month had been the festivities which would be going on this and next week. His first thought was that he wouldn't go to Austin, but one had to obey the summons of a territorial judge.

At four o'clock he turned things over to a deputy and walked the short distance to his new home. To his relief Cassie was there, and he was somewhat dismayed to see that she'd already prepared herself for tonight's dance. The black satiny dress trailed to the floor. The red rose stuck in the low bodice matched the Spanish comb in her hair. She stood in the middle of the living room, waiting expectantly for his smile of approval at her appearance.

"Another new dress," he said curtly.

Casandra moved into the entryway and gazed demurely up into his eyes. "Darling," she said, "all I want to do is please you. Surely you must know that?"

"I guess so," he said sullenly, and hanging his hat on a wall hook

She handed him a twenty dollar gold piece. "Tonight I'm buying my husband supper at the hotel. That is, if it meets with his approval?"

A reluctant grin parted his lips, and he drawled slowly, "You know, I've got the prettiest wife in Texas." From what she'd told him the money she had gotten after her husband had died hadn't been that substantial, so he didn't question her now about the money she'd just given him. Still, it seemed strange that she hadn't paid off the merchants of Waco. "Oh, yes"—he placed an arm around her shoulders—"I have to go to Austin."

"Not now I hope?"

"Have to leave on Wednesday."

"Henry Banner, is there another woman?"

"Nope, Mrs. Banner, there ain't. And there ain't gonna be one, ever."

"Well, if you must go, you must. We'll talk about it later. I've prepared your bath."

"Anyway, Cassie, isn't this dress kind of daring for this town—"

"You do want me to look nice, Henry?"

"It's just that I'll never get a chance to dance with my wife."

"Why, Henry Banner, I do declare you're jealous!" Then she headed him in the direction of the bathroom.

8

Within the hour the marshal of Waco and his wife were strolling along main street and into the soft crimson glow of the October sun sinking toward the upward flow of the distant horizon. From behind came the rapid clop-clop of horses, then a fancy buggy pulled by a team of blacks passed them to draw up further along the street before a variety house. Out of the corners of his eyes, Long Henry was suddenly aware of the merchant Jed Bullock watching them from inside the man's general store. One of his deputies had mentioned that Bullock had sent his wife back east at her insistence, that she was seeking a divorce. Maybe the woman had found out that Bullock was spending a lot of time at the Mex cribs, and at any rate, Long Henry had stayed out of Bullock's way.

Upon entering the Frontier Hotel, Casandra removed the lacy veil and put it in her purse as they found the corridor leading to the dining room. Others were waiting just outside for tables, milling about or seated on overstuffed settees. Easing onto one, Casandra said, "I just love fiddle music."

"What?" Long Henry said, sitting down beside her.

"You're not listening again, Henry. They brought in a fiddler all the way from Abilene . . . and if you don't dance with me . . ."

"Dancing sure ain't one of my strong suits."

"Nonsense." Patting him on the arm, Casandra shifted her eyes covertly to those already seated in the dining room, and to one man in particular. He was Jason McClintock, she knew. Out of Wyoming Territory. His spread, he'd told Casandra, stretched from the Big Horns and to the southeast, over a hundred miles of ranchland. There was no doubt in her mind that she'd dance with McClintock tonight. She hadn't told Marshal Banner that she'd met the rancher last week, had let him take her for a buggy ride this last Saturday morning; yesterday McClintock had treated her to brunch in this very room. Casandra thrilled to the danger of what she was doing.

Craftily she'd drawn the rancher out, learned of his being a widower, and a lonely one at that, knew with a hard intuition that he was the one she'd been seeking all of her life. Jason McClintock, though he didn't know it yet, was going to be her ticket out of here and to a land far, far away where there would be no ghosts out of her past. As for Banner, the marshal of this hot, miserable town, the news that he'd be going to Austin this week simplified matters.

When they were moving into the dining room, Casandra was pleased to see that Jason McClintock was looking her way, and she smiled back with her eyes.

"Somebody you know?"

"Oh, darling," she chided him, and settling onto a chair, "you know how these ranchers are when they're away from home. But I do believe I bumped into that gentleman as I came out of the millinery shop. It . . . it was more embarrassing than anything else."

Long Henry forgot about the matter when their waitress arrived to take their order. During the course of their dinner, other men paid Casandra conpliments with appreciative smiles, and he knew that it was only because of her great beauty. Casandra, in turn, paid strict attention to her meal, and her husband, chatting gaily to Long Henry about household matters or asking him questions about his marshal's job. But she was well aware of Jason McClintock's departure from the dining room.

When they emerged from the Frontier Hotel, main street throbbed with the sounds of night life, and above the brighter glow of street lamps could be seen a sky riddled with stars. Hooking her arm through his, Casandra said huskily, "A penny for your thoughts, my love?"

"Reckon I'm thinking about that trip to Austin."

"Will you miss me?"

He leaned over and kissed her shining black hair. "Still can't believe you're my wife, Cassie. Guess I'm the luckiest man in town."

Then the sound of fiddle music was drawing them into the Yellow Rose dance hall, and out onto its crowded dance floor at Casandra's insistence, with the fiddler who'd come all the way from Abilene breaking out into the Turkey Trot, and with Long Henry clumsily trying to follow Casandra's nimble dance steps.

"Whoa now, woman, this is worse than trying to brand a spooked longhorn."

After a set of dances, they gathered along a wall with others, and Long Henry said, "That's sure tough on a full stomach. Care for something to drink? Some wine?" Nodding, he weaved through the fringe of those crowding the dance floor, went into the barroom and ordered the drinks, and as he stood at the end of the bar listening without much interest to the murmur of voices around him, a deputy entered, saw the marshal and came over.

"Town's building up steam."

"I'll be here if you need me."

"There was a little ruckus over at Goldie's Emporium. Gambler named O'Shay, Deacon O'Shay, was winning big in a poker game."

"Somebody accuse O'Shay of cheating again?"

"Most everybody there, those in the game, told me O'Shay is a square-shooter. It was another player, some gunslinger named Killane who got his dander up. Been hitting the bottle mighty hard. When this gambler told Killane to make his play or vamoose, Killane sort of laughed and left. His going like that don't set right with the man's character. I've got suspicions Killane's up to something."

"You can't arrest a man for suspicions."

Back in the dance hall, Long Henry pulled up short when he saw that Casandra was gone, and he scanned the crowd, then he caught a glimpse of red comb against a black-haired background, and Casandra, talking heatedly to the gunslinger, Navajo Killane. From the way Killane stood Long Henry knew the man was drunk, and now he started forward when Killane grabbed Casandra by the arm, only to have her pull away and hurry across the floor. When he

63

reached her, he asked anxiously, "What did he want?"

"Just another drunk who wanted to dance," she said.

As he passed Casandra her drink, he had the feeling it was more than that, but under the spell of her calm smile there was a moment of reassurance.

"Evening, folks."

"Why," said Casandra, "I do believe you're the man I bumped into the other day. Ah . . . Mr . . ."

"Jason McClintock, ma'am."

"I'm Casandra Banner. My husband, Henry."

Long Henry gazed down at the shorter, older man, noting the pleasant smile on the firm mouth, the crinkles around the steady eyes, and the square face shaped by the elements. A man to be trusted, he decided. McClintock was stolid, with square hands and blunt fingers, and dressed conservatively in a western suit. When McClintock thrust out a hand, Long Henry noticed the gold ring inlaid with a cluster of diamonds before he grasped the hand and shook it firmly.

"McClintock, you said."

"From up Wyoming way. Nice town you've got here."

"Growing," replied Long Henry.

"Would you mind very much if I asked your wife to dance, sir?"

"Not at all," he said, relieved that he wouldn't have to try his hand out on the floor again, because the fiddler had been playing some of that new-fangled music, which according to Casandra, was popular down in New Orleans; Cajun music, she'd called it. McClintock, he noticed, knew his way around a dance floor, while Casandra seemed captivated by the rancher, talking animatedly but managing to follow the man's every move. He turned his attention to the crowd, and when he gazed back at the floor, it was to see Jed Bullock moving through the dancers to Casandra and McClintock. Even from this distance he could see the look of displeasure on Casandra's face, then the ugly tug at Bullock's mouth when she wouldn't allow the man to cut in, and swinging around, Bullock moved stiffly away.

Shortly after midnight the fiddler stopped playing, and Marshal Banner and his wife went home. In the privacy of their bed he reached for her, but Casandra pulled away and said, "It's late, darling, go to sleep."

"I'll miss you when I'm down in Austin."

"We'll talk about it tomorrow," she mumbled.

"Love you."

He waited for her to speak, and when she remained silent, Long Henry turned onto his side away from her and stared into the darkness, wondering what he'd done to make her angry.

9

"That was a stupid play, Navajo!"

The gunslinger, Navajo Killane, lay on the bed in his hotel room, his hands cupped behind his head, a mocking smile on his face. It was Wednesday evening, going on ten o'clock, and a few minutes ago Casandra had slipped into this rundown hotel on the edge of town. Most of her anger was directed at something, she believed, that could jeopardize everything. She was with child by Henry Banner, a situation which should never have happened. In order for her plan to succeed she would have to convince the rancher, Jason McClintock, that the child was his. She had only conceived about a month ago. How could it have happened? As for Killane, he must never know about her pregnancy. If he found out, it would be a weapon that he'd use against her.

"Stupid, huh?" His black eyes narrowed into slits.

"Forget what I called you!" she snapped back, and pacing to a window and looking outside through the dirty panes. She turned around, paced by the bed.

"We're talking about a lot of money here, Navajo."

"Getting hitched to a marshal is what I call doing somethin' stupid."

"Sure," she blazed out. "If you hadn't taken most of my money it wouldn't have happened. I had no choice. Anyway, I figure on leaving here before Banner gets back from Austin."

"All you said in your letter was that you wanted me here, Cassie. So, I'm here?" He motioned toward the dresser. "Hand me that bottle."

"You'll listen to me first, Navajo! For now I want you to lay off the boozing. Here's the way of it. My mark is a rancher named Jason McClintock. He's wealthy. A lonely widower."

"Ain't you forgettin' you got a husband—"

"I want you to kill the marshal!"

Navajo Killane threw Casandra a studious look. It was the way she said it that had gotten to him, as if she'd already forgotten about the man, and he'd bet his last double eagle she had erased completely from her mind any remembrance of what she'd done in New Orleans. She was more Injun than he was, he figured. His teeth flashed golden in a smile, and he said, "Cassie, you've got to be the mother of all she-devils."

"I want it done right after I've left town."

"Yeah," he muttered, and wanting her now. "Come here."

"No!" she hissed. "There's too much at stake for us to get involved now. Can't you see that?" Her present condition had dulled her lust for Killane, and some of the bitterness she felt for him because he'd stolen from her hadn't quite gone away.

"Reckon you must have a real mark here. 'Cause

back in New Orleans you couldn't keep your hands off me. You sure this McClintock is all that rich?" He swung his legs to the floor and sat up.

"I've done some checking here. According to others, McClintock has one of the biggest ranches in Wyoming."

"Must be pretty gullible too, otherwise he wouldn't have fallen for someone like you."

Through a glance she said, "Once you take care of the marshal, I want you to head up to Cheyenne. Stay there until you hear from me."

"What'll you be doing in the meantime?"

"I figure on getting married to McClintock."

"Which will make everything legal-like when he dies. And I reckon we don't have to worry none about his health. 'Cause once you get your hooks into him, it'll take a turn for the worse."

"Must you be so damned vulgar all the time, Navajo!" she cried out.

"Cassie baby, what you're seeing is my sunny disposition. Just don't do nothing to rile me up." He reached to the dresser top for the bottle.

Close like this, Casandra could see the savagery in him, and she fought down the sudden urge to throw herself at him, to feel that hard, demanding body against hers. She glanced away to shield from him the passion burning in her eyes. "Now," she said, and looking his way again, "I want you to manhandle me, give me a black eye."

"Why?"

"Because I want McClintock to believe that I had a fight with my husband, that he slapped me around before he left town. Well, just don't keep on drink—"

68

Without warning, and his face expressionless, he backhanded Casandra across the face. She gasped in pain and tumbled back against the wall. Her knees buckled, and she fell awkwardly to the floor. "Damn you," she moaned through her pain, "you could have warned me!"

Grinning, Killane said, "Just doing what the lady wanted."

Already Casandra could feel her right eye closing as she struggled to her feet, and with Killane still smiling at her. She groped past the dresser to the wash stand, where she dampened a cloth and held it against her face, the pain subsiding now, her head clearing. This was Killane's manner, she pondered, swift and deadly. But if he interfered with her plan, and despite how she felt about him, she would get rid of him. She stared into the broken piece of mirror above the wash stand, realizing that a black eye was a small price to pay for what she hoped to gain. Then she applied some makeup, put on her coat before facing Killane again.

"Well, Navajo, in my letter I said I'd gotten married. Yet you still came here."

"No marriage will keep us apart," he said cockily. "Yeah, I came here to Waco. You're a schemer, Cassie. I figure all I've got to do is trail behind you and pick up a lot of blue chips."

"Then you'll do as I asked?"

"Reckon so. But before you cut out, Cassie baby, I need some hard coin, say a couple of hundred for now."

She opened her purse and took out some money. "All I've got is fifty dollars."

Navajo Killane shrugged with his shoulders as he reached for the money. "It'll do for now. When is the marshal of Waco due back in town?"

"On Sunday. But I'll be long gone before then. Just make sure he's dead!"

On the lower landing Casandra drew the shawl over her head to shield her face as she hurried through the lobby and outside, when the balmy air of night seemed to caress her throbbing eye. No street lamps showed on this quiet street, and now she hurried eastward toward the beckoning lights on main street. If she'd read her man correctly, Navajo Killane would do her bidding. And Casandra had no illusions about how the rancher would react to her unexpected presence when he saw her swollen countenance. There would be the look of outrage, the solicitous words for her, which would be her cue to tell Jason McClintock about her intentions to catch the stage for Abilene, Kansas; and this was exactly what happened when she entered his upstairs rooms in the Frontier Hotel.

"Why go to Abilene? There are plenty of lawyers here."

"Because this is Marshal Banner's town. He'd never give me a divorce." With the handkerchief he'd handed her she dabbed at her eyes.

"That . . . sidewinder!"

"Forget him for now. I . . . I could use a drink . . ."

He rose from where he'd been sitting next to her on the divan and went to the liquor cabinet, where he filled two glasses with brandy. When he turned around, Casandra was there, taking a glass and touching him gently on his ruddy cheek.

"You're so sweet, Jason."

"How can a man do that to you," he said harshly.

"You must remember that my husband is insanely jealous. Why, I've hardly been able to leave the house. I really don't know why I married him, Jason. Living with someone you don't love is . . . pure hell."

They went back to the divan, and sat down, with Jason McClintock placing a comforting arm around her shoulders. "Cassie, you must know that I'm very fond of you. If there's anything I can do, anything at all . . ."

She snuggled deeper into the crook of his arm. "It's such a long and lonely ride to Abilene by stage—"

"I can hire a buggy, take you there."

"That would be marvelous. "But, no, there's your convention."

"I insist upon taking you there, Cassie, and I won't take no for an answer!"

"We'd have to leave before the weekend."

"Consider it done," he said gruffly. He touched his glass to hers. "Here's to your future, Cassie."

"Oh, Jason, how charming."

"I might be a little older than you," he said uncertainly, "but . . ."

"Hush, Jason McClintock. You're in the prime of life. Now, I'd better go before you get the idea I'm a wayward woman."

"Must you leave?"

She rose, as he did, then she handed him the empty glass. "Tomorrow I'll pack my things."

"Renting a buggy presents no problem. We could leave in the morning."

"Oh, Jason," she cried out, and throwing her arms around his neck, "you don't know what this means to me."

"Now, now, Cassie, I can't stand a woman's tears. And I reckon it's best we're leaving tomorrow. Just don't know how I'd control myself if I was still here when the marshal got back." Recklessly, Jason McClintock kissed the beautiful woman he held in his arms, his mind whirling with the thoughts of what Cassie could mean to him if by some remarkable and remote chance she consented to accompany him to Wyoming. The death of his wife some five years ago had left a void in his heart, and batching it was a lonely life.

To a rustle of satin Cassie pulled away. "Until tomorrow then, Jason. I can be ready at sunup. I'm hoping we can leave before . . . before some of his friends see us. They might interfere."

"I understand. Until tomorrow."

In the privacy of her bedroom, Casandra packed into three valises the clothing she'd selected, while on the floor around the bed were garments she had discarded. The excitement of what was to come revealed itself in her eyes, and in the bright flushing of her face. Through the open door circulated heat from the wood-burning fireplace, but some of the color in her cheeks was caused by the brandy she'd been drinking while packing. She wore a lacy chemise, slippers on her feet, her long hair spilling carelessly over bare shoulders. She pressed a hand against her stomach, thinking that perhaps her present condition was a blessing in disguise. It was a considerable distance to Abilene, Kansas, with several nightly stops along the way, and despite their differences in age, the rancher might prove to be a virile lover once he succumbed to her charms.

She stiffened in alarm at the sound of the front door being opened, and now at the tread of footsteps in the hallway, and hurriedly she donned a robe and darted over to the dresser to reach into a drawer for a small derringer. It could be Navajo, she reasoned, but knowing his nature knew that he'd be involved in a poker game about this time of night. The presence of the gun stilled some of the fear, and she called out. "Who's there?"

"An old friend," came a man's voice.

What was Jed Bullock doing here? Could be that he came over to apologize for his behavior at the dance. On her trips downtown, she'd been well aware of his watchful eyes, and a couple of times Bullock had purposely gone out of his way to talk to her. Bullock would only come here if he knew that her husband wasn't in town. She hid the gun under a pillow on the bed, checked her appearance in the dresser mirror before going into the living room. Something about the way he was staring at her caused alarm bells to go off in Casandra's head.

Bullock tossed his hat on an overstuffed chair, advanced further into the living room. "You don't look happy that I'm here."

She said cautiously: "What do you want?"

"You," he said.

"How dare you come here, Mr. Bullock!"

"The high and mighty Mrs. Banner," he retorted. "Here you are, pretending to be someone you ain't."

"What are you talking about?"

"Our esteemed marshal would sure like to hear

73

about New Orleans."

Casandra paled, sagged against the table, and watched helplessly as Bullock reached into an inner coat pocket and produced a piece of paper, which he unfolded and held up for her to see. "The whore Casandra Ashbury is wanted for murder! And the picture is almost an exact likeness."

"You . . . bastard!" she started toward her bedroom, only to have Bullock leap forward and grab her arm.

"Not so fast, my lovely," he said bitterly. With his other hand he fastened onto a hunk of her hair and drew her close. "This can be our little secret if you do exactly as I say."

"What do you mean?"

"Damn you, Cassie, I knew I was going to bed you the moment you stepped off that stage. And I generally get what I go after, whore." In his need to have her Jed Bullock had forgotten that he'd dropped the reward poster, but even if he had noticed it, the sight of her in the dark red chemise drove all reason from his mind. "Your husband give you that black eye? Or another lover?"

Casandra knew that it would be useless to make an outcry. Somehow she had to get him into her bedroom, for her only chance was the derringer. She spat into his face, laughed mockingly. "You'll never get away with this! Never!"

Her outburst seemed to fan Bullock's lust, and savagely he kissed her on the neck, the bare shoulder, leaving faint teeth marks. She offered no resistance as he picked her up and found her bedroom. On the wide bed was a valise, and he kicked it to the floor, saying, "Going on a trip, whore?" He threw her onto the bed.

"From now on I'm calling the shots. You'll not be leaving this town, hear! Now, it's about time that you had a real man." Discarding his coat and shirt, he unbuckled his belt and began removing his trousers while sneering down at her.

Casandra stretched out on the bed as though she realized getting away was futile, the expression on her face that of a woman who'd just been mastered. Her arms lifted above her head to fall back on the pillows, but slowly, her eyes riveted to his lust-filled face, she brought her left hand down and under the pillow, where it curled around the derringer. Then, hatred smoldering in her eyes, she pointed the weapon at Bullock's chest and pulled the trigger. The sharp crack of the weapon was followed by his cry of surprise, and he staggered backward.

"Damn you!" he snarled. He came forward, but Casandra scrambled from the bed to run past his reaching hands for the living room. Now Bullock's only thought was to get his own revolver out of his coat, and palming it, he stumbled after her, with the room spinning, fighting a limb-sapping weakness.

Casandra fled into the kitchen, found a butcher knife and moved back to stand beside the door leading into the living room. He saw her there, fired wildly in her direction, and then his body came unhinged and he fell against the door. He lost his grip on the gun as he dropped to the floor, still conscious, and grimly aware of Casandra coming toward him, the steely blade of the butcher knife catching the reflecting glare coming from the fireplace. This was a murderess coming for him, Jed Bullock's brain screamed, as the fingers of his left hand clawed desperately toward his own weapon. When the knife plunged into Bullock's back, he stiffened in shock, and the last thing his gaping eyes saw was the face of Casandra Ashbury on the reward poster.

Casandra's hand came away from the handle of the butcher knife and she fell away from the body. She sat on the floor for a moment, drawing great draughts of air into her lungs, and letting the fear pounding at her temples go away. Now her only concern was that the shots had been heard from nearby houses. Springing up from the floor, she hurried to the front door and peered out into the darkness. Much to her relief no inquisitive lights showed through dark windows, and if anybody had heard the gunfire, they would put it down to nothing more than a drunken cowhand having a go at a good time.

Back in her bedroom, Casandra steadied her trembling hands as she filled a glass with brandy. She drank about half of its fiery contents. The brandy settled her down some, and the first name that came to mind was Navajo Killane's. He must help her get rid of the body. As she dressed, the flame in the lamp gave her another idea, and she murmured thoughtfully, "It would be safer to leave the body here, set fire to the house." The only complication, she foresaw was of Jason McClintock coming here in the morning. She could drag the body down into the basement, start a fire when she saw McClintock's buggy coming down the street, and by the time any flames showed, they'd be well on their way to Abilene.

After fortifying her nerves by drinking another glass of brandy, Casandra turned her attention to Jed Bullock. First she pulled out his billfold, where to her surprise she came up with around three hundred dollars. Then she grabbed the outstretched arms and dragged the body over to the door opening onto the basement staircase. She was sweating by the time she got the upper part of the body on the top steps, and bracing herself against the door frame, she shoved with her feet against his legs, and then the body was rolling and clumping to the bottom of the steps. She lit a lamp, went into the basement, and piled old boards and broken pieces of cabinetry left by the previous tenants into a pile that reached to within a few feet of the wooden floor boards. Upon rising tomorrow morning, the first thing she'd have to do would be to slip down here with some lamps and empty what kerosene they contained onto the wood. She edged around the body and hurried upstairs and into her bedroom

Whether it was the effect of the brandy, or the fact that she'd killed before, Casandra undressed calmly, unhurriedly, almost forgetting about the presence of Jed Bullock's body in the basement. She put curlers into her hair, wanting to look her best for the rancher, humming to herself as she did so. Bullock, she realized, had been of some use to her after all, because after they found the charred remains of his body, everyone would believe that she had died in the fire.

But somehow Navajo Killane would sense that she was still alive, and head up to Cheyenne after killing the marshal. On the other hand, with everyone here believing that she was dead, she could find Killane tonight and tell him not to gun down Henry Banner. She turned out the lamp, crawled into bed, tucked the covers up around her, and smiled at the moonlight beaming against the bedroom windows. No, the marshal had to die. Then, by a trick of her mind, it was difficult for Casandra to recall what her husband looked like, for she'd already consigned him to the past. And with a smile still gracing her lips Casandra fell into a peaceful sleep.

10

The stagecoach veered around a freight wagon and drew up in front of the Wells Fargo office. The last passenger to emerge was Long Henry, and he smiled at Doc Sam Holter, there to meet him. The agent handed him his only piece of luggage, then he said, "Doc, I sure could use a cup of java. That was a cold ride."

"I'm afraid you'll need something stronger than that, Henry."

He followed Doc Holter to the lee of the building and out of the biting wind. "Another killing?"

"Henry, your house burned down early Thursday morning."

"Cassie?" Then from the look on Doc Holter's face he knew that something had happened to his wife.

"We found her body in the basement. Henry, I'm sorry."

Long Henry leaned against the wall for support, not wanting to believe that Cassie was dead. This was too unreal, something that happened to others. "I shouldn't have gone to Austin."

"You can't blame yourself, Henry. The fire seems to

have started in the basement."

"You said you found her body there," he said.

"It was found there."

"Cassie hated the sight of the basement, never went down there."

"I was wondering about that too, Henry. It appeared that someone had piled up the debris in the basement, set fire to it." Now he told Long Henry that Jed Bullock hadn't been seen since Wednesday night, and then in a local saloon. "Do you want to take a look at what's left of the house?"

Nodding that he did, Long Henry fell into step with Holter. His brow furrowed in thought. Bullock had been sweet on Casandra, had been the first man she'd gone out with here. The man's wife had gone back east, and it could be that Bullock had designs on Casandra, though she didn't seem to want to have anything to do with the man. There was always the possibility that Bullock knew about his leaving town and had gone over to see Casandra. He voiced this to Holter as the charred remains of the house came into view, and they stopped out in the street.

"I hate to think about making funeral arrangements," Long Henry said sadly.

"I want you to hold off on that, Henry. Just between us now, the body was burned pretty badly. But that's what troubles me. The fact that we found only the one body. Supposing Bullock did go to your house Wednesday night . . . and just supposing that it was his body we found . . ."

"You mean . . . you mean Cassie could still be alive?" Hope flared in Long Henry's eyes. "The fire was set deliberately. But by whom? And why? Yeah,

Sam, as marshal I had some enemies, some I sent to the territorial prison. But killing a woman just don't seem to fit their styles. More'n likely someone would bushwhack me."

"All that was left were a few bones and the skull. Was your wife seeing a dentist?"

"Anyways, not here. Seemed to have good teeth."

"The teeth in the skull, Henry, contained several fillings. I took the liberty of going over to Bullock's house and looking through his papers. Found out that he'd been going to a dentist down in Austin on a regular basis. The man wasn't that much taller than your wife, so the other bones don't help us much. The only way we can make a positive identification is to send for that dentist. I've taken care of that."

"But if Cassie's alive?"

"Where is she?" Doc Holter fished out a flask, unscrewed the cap and passed it to Long Henry. At this point in time he didn't want to voice his opinions about Casandra to a man he considered a close friend. But the way he had it figured was that she'd had a hand in the murder of the merchant, Jed Bullock. There wasn't any way of proving this, as no man alive could point out the source of the wind, or the workings of the universe, and it was his notion that he'd been right about Casandra being that flowered cactus; beautiful to behold, deadly to the touch.

"Well," Long Henry said wearily, and turning to move back along the street, "no sense building my hopes up."

Doc Holter replaced the flask in his coat pocket. "You're bunking at my place for now, Henry."

"Appreciate it. Any killings or robbings while I was

gone?"

"A few fights."

"Maybe I should check in at the jail."

"Do that tomorrow," Doc Holter said firmly. "What we both need is a good steak and some whiskey under our belts."

Long Henry knew that he would cling to the hope that his wife was still alive. Life without Cassie would have little meaning. She must have been kidnapped. And if Jed Bullock had gone over there, he could have blundered in when the kidnappers were still there, been killed because he went lusting after another man's wife.

11

When Doc Holter opened the curtains, afternoon sunlight spilled across the desk in his cluttered office. Medical books filled two cabinets, with some piled on his desk, some of the tools of his trade lay on a table, and though Holter had gone to an eastern medical school, no framed diplomas hung from the painted walls.

Long Henry was there, along with the dentist from Austin, a sparse, taciturn man, who preferred nodding to talking, and sat across from Long Henry at the desk while probing at the teeth in the skull with a metal instrument.

"Interesting," he finally muttered, and it seemed a lengthy stretch of time to the others before he spoke again, and with the words coming out with a grudging slowness. "My work."

"It is," said a relieved Long Henry, and pointing at the skull, "or was Jed Bullock?"

"What I said—Bullock."

"Seems I was right," commented Holter, as he leaned

back in his swivel chair and steepled his hands before him.

"Doctor Alderman, I'd appreciate your keeping this between us."

"Can do, Marshal Banner." The dentist gathered up his instruments, placed them in a black bag, and reached for his hat. "Good day, gentlemen."

Doc Holter escorted the dentist to the open door, closed it after the man had crossed over the threshold, found a bottle of whiskey and settled behind his desk again. "Anyway, part of what happened has been solved. Care to join me?"

"It'll go down a lot easier now that I know Cassie is still alive." Long Henry rose, began pacing the floor. Inside, there was a feeling of elation. But churning within his mind were questions that he needed answers to. Casandra had not left on the stage, nor had she been seen leaving with anyone else. The fire, he'd found out, had started around sunrise and before others living nearby were up. The murder of Jed Bullock, Casandra's disappearance, these facts were troubling enough, but it was the lack of clues that troubled him. It was as if his wife had simply vanished into thin air. Ever since Monday morning he and his deputies had been asking questions around town, and with no answers forthcoming.

"No sense working up to an ulcer, Henry."

In the days to come Marshal Banner knew with a grim certainty that he'd made absolutely no progress toward finding his wife. She could be dead for all he knew, murdered by the same person or persons who killed Bullock. He found it hard to perform his duties, and he settled within himself, letting his deputies do most of the work. A week passed, and his usual vigilance wasn't there when he made his rounds at night, not checking the alleys or cross streets in passing, and rarely speaking to those he encountered on the streets.

On a weekday Long Henry had a few beers in a saloon, topping that off with a shot of rotgut before continuing on his rounds. There was a stubble of beard showing, and he'd worn the same clothes for three days running. When he came to a street corner, he paused carelessly in the full glow of a street lamp and rolled a cigarette. The streets were unusually quiet, the colder days keeping most of the townspeople indoors at night, the dark sky overcast, and building up to storm, he figured. As he touched flame to a wooden match by striking it on his metal belt buckle, a flicker of movement came to him from the deeper blackness across the bisecting streets, and he stared that way, trying to pick it up again.

After a while he tossed the match away, inhaled on the cigarette and mumbled indiffernetly, "Probably another drunk."

The first bullet struck him high in the chest before he heard the harsh roll of the rifle reverberating down the street. The impact spun him around, and he fell against a bench resting along the facade of the building. Gasping in pain, the cigarette dropped from his mouth as he reached to pull out his revolver.

Pow!

Another slug slammed into his side, spinning him around, dropping him to the boardwalk. His revolver hit and bounced away. Now vividly clear in his memory were the same sensations he'd felt when he'd been wounded at Gettysburg, but this was a deeper, a killing pain, He knew that his only chance to survive this was to crawl around the corner of the building, and by then one of his deputies or some townspeople would have heard the shots and come to investigate them.

Desperately he pushed to his knees, only to fall back onto his side, dimly aware of movement further downstreet as a few people pushed outside, but closer, and from across the intersection appeared the dim outline of a man holding a Winchester. The sound of a shell being levered into its breech came to Long Henry, and with all of his remaining strength he forced his weakening frame and outstretched arm closer to his revolver.

The bushwhacker jumped up onto the boardwalk and kicked the weapon away from Long Henry's closing fingers. "Nice night for a killing," the man said coldly, and flashing a golden smile, though hatred blazed out of his greenish eyes. In that brief shock-filled moment the marshal of Waco recognized that it was the gunslinger, Navajo Killane, knew the next bullet was going to slam into his head.

"This is from an old friend."

Again Navajo Killane's teeth flashed golden in the pale glow of the street lamp as he laughed, and he brought the barrel of his rifle to bear on Long Henry's forehead.

"Hey!" someone shouted. Then a bullet thudded into the wall close to Killane.

Navajo Killane snapped a hurried shot off down at the fallen marshal, and whirled away to lose himself in the darkness, and back where he'd just been. It felt to

Long Henry that his throat had been ripped away. He reached a feeble hand there in a vain attempt to stem the flow of blood, and then he was descending into a black pit.

12

Once again Long Henry was aware of that harsh sound, a creak, creak, as of crickets chirping along a stream; that, and a cool breeze touching his bare arms and face. His eyes fluttered open, and after they'd focused, he gazed in disinterest at Doc Holter seated in a rocking chair facing his bed. Only Long Henry's eyes moved, but slowly in their sockets, and with pain seeming to sweep away from them and grip his chest and throat. He was floating, disembodied somehow, and so lightheaded that the ceiling lamp looked as if it were up near the clouds.

"Welcome back, Henry."

The voice had a hollow ring to it, nor did the words, "welcome back," have any meaning, for he had no recollection of what had happened, and wearied now by the exertion of opening his eyes, he drifted off to sleep.

When he awakened again it was to find that the ceiling lamp had been lit, and though he was alone, from nearby came the comforting sound of voices. And with this awareness came also bits and fragments of what had happened that night — his own carelessness, rifle fire followed by pain, that awful helplessness he'd felt when Navajo Killane stood over him. He tried to turn his head, raise an arm, movements that brought on instant agony. But at least he was alive, and this was all that mattered, or was it, for with consciousness came thoughts of Casandra.

Through the open doorway appeared Doc Holter and Bill Tilwell, a deputy, who said cheerfully, "Marshal, according to the doc here, you're gonna pull through."

Stepping around the bed, Holter placed a hand on his patient's forehead. "Well, the fever's broken. Henry, you've got the constitution of an ox; otherwise you'd have cashed in your chips. Hungry?"

Long Henry opened his mouth to respond, but to his dismay all that passed through his parched lips was a raspy croaking sound. His questing eyes fixed on Doc Holter's face.

Holter ran a hand along his rumpled hair. Then, as if he'd just come to a momentous decision, he said gently, "Henry, I figure I've got to level with you. For starters, the wounds in your chest and side are healing nicely. But it's the one to your throat that has me concerned. That slug messed up your larynx . . . or in layman's terms your voice box. It's healing too, but there's some question as to whether or not you'll be able to talk again . . ." His voice broke some when he added, "I did everything in my power, Henry, but now it's in the hands of a higher authority."

It took a few minutes for what Doc Holter had said to infiltrate into Long Henry's thoughts, and then when he realized what this meant, panic widened his eyes, followed by a terrible anger at the man who'd bushwacked him, and the thunderous, damning words that filled his mind begged to come out screaming through his mouth. The moment of rage passed, to be replaced by thoughts of vengeance so great that his clenched teeth seemed to splinter from the hard pressure he'd placed upon them.

"For now," went on Holter, "I'm just thankful that you're alive. As for your throat, time has a way of healing most things."

Nearly a month passed before Long Henry was able to hobble about Doc Holter's house, which was set off by itself behind a row of poplars. The days had cooled more, as had his vengeful anger. The only woman he'd ever loved was gone forever, he felt. As for Killane, he could find no reason why the man would gun him down. Unless, as Doc Holter had stated, someone wanted him out of the way. Close by the house, and angling off to the northwest, was a creek almost barren of water, and with brush growing along it, and he came here at times to search for some answers to what had happened.

He became resigned to the silence of his thoughts. On occasion he'd try, and fail, to utter any words. Waco, he realized, sure as sin couldn't use a marshal who was a mute, and he turned in his letter of resignation. Most of the money he received for being marshal he gave to Doc Holter over the man's protests.

And one December day he woke up, knowing that it was time to move on again.

"Henry, take care. You're going to try and find her, aren't you?"

Nodding, he shook the outstretched hand and swung aboard his horse. He wheeled the horse around and loped it down a westward-running lane. Even though Doc Holter stood there until he was out of sight, Long Henry never looked back, setting his mind and sights in the direction he'd chosen. A few days back it had come to him loud and clear that his wife was still alive. Where would she go? Certainly not up north, for she'd told him once that she hated cold weather. So for no particular reason he had decided to head this way, with no apparent destination in mind, only a notion to look for her, and the whole, wide west spread out before him.

PART TWO

13

The pair of riders came cautiously through Red Canyon in the Black Hills, pushed along by a blustery wind, and warily scanning the high rims. Ahead and in the growing dimness of twilight lay Deadwood, and sweeping in from the south was a v-shaped flock of Canada geese, passing above the rims of the canyon like storm-borne leaves, heading north as if invisibly tethered to one will, and arriving late in the season, thought Long Henry. But they flew with a fixed destination in mind, where they'd summer. If only he had wings he'd join them, forget about searching for the woman he'd loved and lost.

Gray was showing in his hair now, around the temples and sideburns, and after seven years of wandering throughout the west in search of his wife he was tempered to a hard leanness, a hard glitter in his eyes, and with his somber face weathered by the elements.

"Just about through," said Deacon O'Shay. "Maybe the outlaws who infest these parts are taking a day off." They'd been warned that Red Canyon was the scene of many holdups, and though they seemed to be alone, O'Shay still kept his Winchester balanced before him on the saddle. Dangling from his compressed lips was a cigarillo. Deacon O'Shay could be forty, then again older. Deep lines grooved his swarthy face, and his cynical black eyes seemed to say that he'd seen what life had to offer and hadn't been too impressed by it. He wore a duster over his frock coat, and he rode with the easy elegance of a man used to spending long hours in the saddle. From his Irish father he'd inherited an easy smile and a voice that could break out into song or charm with words those he played poker with, while the Mex part of him showed in his dark looks and cynical nature.

Clearing the pass without incident, they rode at a lope along the stagecoach road winding among jagged spires and tree-stippled hills. Though it wanted to break out into a gallop, Long Henry kept a tight rein on his rangy hammerhead, being in no mood for a faster gait because of the dull throbbing coming from his throat. Once in a while he'd reach under his bandana and rub the edges of the scar mark there. Maybe three weeks, a month ago, he'd gotten into a fight with a local cowhand down in one of those nameless Nebraska towns. The hand, one of those banty rooster types with quick fists, had gotten in a couple of punches before Long Henry had hammered the man into the sawdust. One of the blows had struck him in the throat, and the next morning he'd awoken with it swollen and aching.

"Just my luck," he had mumbled silently, only to hear to his shocked surprise those words coming out

96

raspy and strange sounding, but the first words he'd been able to utter audibly in seven years. Not wanting to build up his hopes, nor O'Shay's, just in case this was only a temporary remedy, he only tried talking when he was alone, forming words, saying whatever his thought was at the moment. And when he had uttered her name, "Cassie," . . . again, and again, the empty place in his heart was almost more than he could bear.

"These gold miners are swimming in money," said O'Shay around his cigarillo. "According to my calculations, we should be getting close to Deadwood." It was their custom to ride in separately, and he went on, "Want me to head in first?"

"We'll flip . . . for it."

The cigarillo dropped from O'Shay's mouth as he drew up sharply. "I'll be go to . . ."

"Remem . . . ber that fight I had . . . down in . . . Nebraska . . ."

"You can talk!" Removing his low-crowned hat, O'Shay scratched at his hair.

"Not too good yet." Long Henry pulled out a silver dollar. "Call it."

"You can talk?"

"Some. Heads or tails?"

"Dammit," exploded Deacon O'Shay, "for going on four years now I've been doing the palavering for two men. All the way up here from Nebraska, pardner, you've been letting me talk . . . letting me answer myself." He began swearing in Spanish, gesturing wildly with his arms, and causing his mount to turn around nervously. "Knowing all the while you could talk."

"Like I said, pardner," Long Henry said uncertainly, "this came on . . . suddenlike. Could be that it ain't all . . . that . . . that permanent. Deacon, for now . . . let's go on as before . . ."

"Reckon you've got your reasons for not wanting anyone to know," said O'Shay. "Okay, I'll take heads."

"Tails." Grinning, Long Henry touched spurs to his horse and cantered on ahead, leaving a smiling and wondering Deacon O'Shay behind.

About a mile out of Deadwood the sky opened and it began raining, and Long Henry put on his slicker. The road he traveled along curled upward following the higher shoulders of the pass. When he reached the summit, and in the harsh glare of lightning, he could see the raw mining town spread out below along the bottom of a deep and narrow canyon. He had never been this far north before, and only now at Deacon O'Shay's insistence. They'd stay just long enough to build up their stake.

He'd encountered O'Shay down in the Cherokee Strip. At the time his possibles consisted of what he could pack on a horse and ten silver dollars, some of which he lost to O'Shay in a poker game. It was his thought then to try to hire on with a trail herd that was passing through, but O'Shay suggested that they team up, that he'd teach Long Henry the rudiments of becoming a professional gambler.

He let the hammerhead pick its own way down the road spotted with chuckholes, its clayey surface slickened by the rainwater. At the first fork in the road, he veered to his right, drawn that way by the greater amount of street lamps and by the carved head of a horse he noticed on the stone wall of a livery stable. He rode inside through the open doors and dismounted. After his horse was stabled, he slung the saddlebags over his shoulder and went in search of a lodging place.

Deadwood, he'd heard, had over sixty saloons, and numerous gambling houses and theaters, and some crooked gamblers, but Long Henry and his partner always played a square game. Winning was just a matter of knowing when to fold or raise, he'd learned. Despite the rain, Main Street was busy, and when lightning flared, he caught a glimpse of buildings clinging precariously to the sloping canyon walls. It was their custom to check into the best hotel in town. The Merchant's Hotel, an imposing stone structure, drew him across the muddy street. In the lobby, he spoke quietly to the clerk on duty. "Your best room."

"About all we've got left is a suite."

"It'll do. Is there someone who can press some clothes?"

"We'll take care of it."

Upstairs in the suite, he handed the clothes he wanted pressed to the clerk, who left, and removing his wet clothing, Long Henry went into the bathroom and eased tiredly into the tub. Then he shaved, and upon moving back into the bedroom, found that his clothes had been pressed. Sometimes when he lingered in a hotel room the ghostly presence of his wife would enter his thoughts, and he dressed quickly. Downstairs, he explored the many corridors in the hotel, to find several billiard parlors and display rooms, and a large dining room, which he entered and sat down at a table. He ate slowly, then lingered over a third cup of coffee while gazing out through a window at people stirring along main street.

From here they would go to St. Louis in his attempt to find Casandra. She'd be a lover of big cities, was his notion. This endless wandering in search of her was getting to Long Henry, aging him, making his mind center, not only on her, but the gunslinger, Killane. Why hadn't he run across the man? Navajo Killane had quite a reputation down along the border states, and in his search there, Long Henry couldn't find one person who'd seen Killane for the past few years. Maybe if he got lucky here and made a sizable poke, he should forget about the past and buy a ranch someplace. Then, sighing in frustration, he left a tip for the waitress, paid his bill at the counter, and went in search of Deacon O'Shay and a poker game.

As if the emergence of Long Henry from the hotel was some kind of signal, it stopped raining. He walked slowly through the narrow streets, somewhat surprised at the number of establishments catering to the gold miners, because there seemed to be as many houses of prostitution as saloons. If some sickness didn't waylay a miner, he reckoned, the unsavory characters living in this wide-open town would separate the man from his gold poke before the night was over. The town sure lived up to Deacon O'Shay's brag.

He entered a small saloon calling itself Hob Jim's Place, and checking the gambling action, saw that all

100

three tables were busy. Moving on down the street, his cursory check of others, the Derby, the Bella Union, the Last Chance, revealed faro banks, Keno layouts, three-card monte, chuck-a-luck, and going on to The Bogeda, a saloon a cut above the average, he came across a roulette wheel that had but a single zero, and knew it was of European style, and because of this figured it was run honest, so he found a place at the bar. He was in no particular hurry to find his partner, knowing O'Shay to be a take-your-time kind of person, and he'd be lingering over supper someplace. As a barkeep placed a whiskey bottle and shot glass before him on the bar, a woman eased up to Long Henry.

"Ain't seen you around here, honey."

He smiled down at her. Though she was pretty in a jaded sort of way, tonight his mind was on other things, and he said softly, "I'll buy you a drink, then I have to go."

"Keep your money, sport," she said testily, and went in search of someone else.

He turned back to his drink. The words were coming out easier now, but the years of silence had ingrained in him a cautiousness, that silence also shielding from others the kind of man he was. To get the lay of this town he could strike up a conversation with those around him, and maybe it was that same wary manner which had prompted him to tell O'Shay to keep from others this newfound ability to speak. The woman he'd just spoken to, the barkeep, would forget him as soon as he left. In some of the places he'd been over the last seven years, people had pointed him out as the former marshal of Waco, telling too of his handicap. Though he resented this, he'd gotten used to it, and on the way up from Nebraska and through the Black Hills, he couldn't shake the feeling that up here he'd meet someone from his past. Anyway, he figured, habits were hard to break.

Outside on Main Street, Long Henry merged with the passersby, most miners, but a few cowhands and townspeople were in evidence. His walks took Long Henry south on Lee to Broadway Street, where more saloons seemed to do a thriving business. In the other mining towns he'd been in further west the miners lived from day to day, were willing to risk all they had at gambling, with the idea in mind that tomorrow, or next week, they'd strike that mother lode. Some of them would be broke or even dead by morning, done in by a prostitute or pickpocket or petty thief. And lurking in the Black Hills were robber gangs, O'Shay had told him.

After looking for his partner in the Nuttall & Mann saloon, and going next door to the Bella Union Theater, a more gaudy barroom, he wandered back up to Main Street to pause at a corner and fish out the makings. Then, Long Henry came alert, gripped as he was by an overpowering premonition of unease; briefly to him came the sounds of shellfire, the acrid scent of gunpowder. He scanned the faces of those passing by, turned his attention to the opposite boardwalk.

"Casandra wouldn't come to a place like this," he murmured quietly. But the former marshal of Waco knew that someone else from his past, possibly Navajo Killane himself, was in town. Though the rain had freshened the air, it also brought to Long Henry the smell of danger. And he would welcome whatever came.

Fashioning a cigarette, and dragging smoke into his lungs, he moved on, and drawn across the rain-gleaming boardwalk to a place called The Lobby because of a large, ornate sign that read, The Lobby — It Leads, Others Follow — Best Brands of Goods, Fine Music, and an Orderly House. As Long Henry passed inside, he was unaware of the two men who'd been watching him from across and further west along the street.

"Heard rumors he was alive."

"Who was that hombre?"

"Thought I'd killed him down in Waco," murmured Navajo Killane, and more to himself than to Vince Talbot, one of the cowhands who'd accompanied him here to Deadwood. Both men worked for Jason Mc-Clintock's MC ranch, out Buffalo, Wyoming way. When things were slack, Killane and a few men he trusted would cut out, come here to the Black Hills and join forces with one of the outlaw gangs infesting these parts. Killane, Talbot, the other hands, were hard men, and most of them had sent someone to Boot Hill. For Navajo Killane it was a way of life that suited his cold and savage nature. He looked hard at Talbot.

"Keep an eye on that man," he ordered.

"Knowing his name would help some," Talbot countered.

"Banner used to be marshal of Waco."

"Yeah, the one they call Long Henry. A mute, I've heard," Talbot laughed mirthlessly.

"Don't let on you're watching him, Talbot."

103

"Reckon you want to kill him yourself, then?"

Navajo Killane stared thoughtfully beyond the other man, realizing that Banner couldn't have shown up at a better time. His being here could only mean that the rumors must be true that he was still looking for his wife. And he was just the man that could lead Banner to the beauteous Casandra McClintock. Being a cattle baron's wife had changed her, and Killane sensed that her future plans didn't include him. Old Jason McClintock put a lot of store in his wife, loved her more than anything else he owned, and it was certain in Killane's mind that McClintock wouldn't take his word that he'd shot the marshal of Waco at Casandra's insistence. There was the boy, too, and bearing little resemblance to McClintock. One thing for sure, now that Killane had actually seen Henry Banner, the woman he'd married was a bigamist, and the gunslinger laughed that crazy laugh of his, knowing that he'd just been dealt four aces to Casandra McClintock's full house. He'd give away all the gold in the Black Hills just to see her face when she found out about Banner. What he intended doing wasn't clear yet in Navajo Killane's mind, but for now the former marshal of Waco was worth more to him alive than dead. Yup, strange how the turnings of life were.

"Don't let him out of your sight, Talbot," he said chillingly, "Or you'll answer to me."

Crossing the street, and cussing some at the mud that splattered his boots, Navajo Killane went downstreet to the Green Front Theater, a large two-story building. Out front, he stared back the way he'd just walked, and satisfied that he wasn't being followed, he shouldered inside. The sign out front stated that the Green Front was the home of burlesque, vaudeville and drama, but it was actually the toughest saloon in town, and Killane felt at home here. The lights were dim, with a pall of smoke hanging near the ceiling, the piano or banjo music loud, and the place reeked of stale beer and other unsavory aromas. Moving along the long bar, he smiled at some of the prostitutes he knew, but favored a dusky woman from the south over the others. He settled down in one of the box stalls. Almost immediately, a barmaid brought over a bottle of the whiskey he liked, and as she went away, a burly man rose from where he'd been seated with four other men at a table and approached Killane.

"Didn't expect you until tomorrow," Nate Winger said curtly, as he eased across the table from Killane. He had runny eyes, and what appeared to be a two day's stubble of beard on his pitted face. At the corner of his down-turned mouth was a round wooden toothpick, and the handlebar mustache needed trimming.

"I like to surprise people." He drank the contents of the shot glass, filled it again. "Any word about that gold shipment?"

Winger stared in surprise at the gunslinger, then nervously scratched at his jawline. "How'd you find out about that?"

"From a certain bank employee."

"Fairwell?"

"Fairwell, head teller of the Merchants National Bank. The bank is shipping out around a half-million in gold bullion."

"What he told me!" exploded Winger. "I paid that

chiseling thief plenty for that information. He was to get back to me later this week about the day of the shipment. I'll tan his cheatin'—"

"Just trying to make a buck, is all," Killane said calmly.

"No sense you and your men getting involved in this."

"If we don't, you'll never pull it off. All you've got for a crew are some alkies, petty thieves and ex-cons, and none of them can shoot worth a damn. As for you, Nate, your memory is about as short as dry grass."

Nate Winger felt the fear rise again. He'd never met a man like the breed before, and though Winger had committed his share of crimes, he knew that he was no match for Navajo Killane when it came to cold-blooded killing. Winger could count on the fingers of one hand the number of holdups he'd pulled off before Killane arrived, and most of them were freight wagons or lone travelers, but afterwards, and with Killane assuming command, they centered their activities around Red Canyon. Winger had an available supply of money now, had the pick of the girls here at the Green Front, but he hated the gunslinger, would kill the man if the opportunity ever presented itself.

"That last job you pulled—"

Winger bristled. "What about it?"

"I hear you got near five thousand from that stage holdup. I want my share."

"But you wasn't there, Navajo!" Winger said hotly.

There was a blur of movement, then Killane's revolver was centered on Nate Winger. "My share, partner!"

"All right," he said through gritted teeth, "guess I didn't understand things." He pulled out a leather pouch and dropped it by Killane's whiskey bottle. "That breaks me, Killane."

"Figures," said Killane, and pushing the pouch toward Winger. "This time I'll let you keep it. And you'll need some more, to buy what supplies and weapons we'll need." He reached to his leather vest pocket and lifted out several double eagle pieces, let them clatter onto the table. "There's too much at stake here to argue over nickels and dimes. Keep your men out at the hideout until we pull this off."

"How about yours?"

"They can handle their booze . . . and mouths. What else did that bank teller let you know about the bullion shipment?"

"They ain't going through Red Canyon. When they get to Hat Creek Station, they'll take the north route to Cheyenne. The bullion will be divided among five wagons."

"Which means they'll be able to travel faster."

"Yup. And they'll be armed to the teeth." Then, Nate Winger explained the plan he had in mind, and to his surprise Killane nodded in acceptance of it.

"Sounds good, Nate. But I figure we'll need an equalizer. Come on."

They went out back and along quiet back streets and alleys until they reached a rundown shack situated on the outskirts of town. Only when they were close to the front door could light be seen seeping through some cracks. Killane rapped on the weatherbeaten panes, and when the door swung open, Nate Winger looked in worried puzzlement at a man wearing the uniform of a soldier. "What kind of game is this?" Winger asked.

"I've bought weapons from Lew Pickett before," Killane explained, moving inside.

"Just been removed from the active duty rolls at Fort Meade," said Pickett, "by way of a bad conduct discharge."

And now Winger saw that the chevrons and buttons had been torn from the man's blue tunic, and in place of the standard issue .45 Pickett wore a holstered Dragoon. Entering, Winger closed the door. "Now I suppose you want to join my gang."

"Pickett's more or less done that," said Killane. He moved around the rickety table to where a tarp was spread over a large object, and when he removed the tarp, he revealed to Winger a gleaming brass Gatling gun and several boxes of shells.

"If that don't beat all," marveled Winger.

"I can get you a howitzer," volunteered Pickett, "or maybe you'd be wanting a field gun."

Winger glared at the man. "You ever fired one of those things?"

"This here child was with General Kettermann helping to round up hostile Sioux and Blackfeet. I got me my share, I did." He spat tobacco juice near Winger's scuffed boots, challenged the man with flinty eyes.

"This'll give us the odds, Nate."

A grudging smile tugged at Winger's mouth. "Reckon it'll be plain murder."

Navajo Killane laughed with the others. "To me it'll be more like a business transaction." Hard cash, he'd

108

come to realize after a lifetime of not having enough of it, determined who was the cock of the walk. He'd seen what it had done to Casandra, knew she was drifting away from him, though he still went to her bedroom from time to time. But one of these days she'd turn on him. Lately, she'd been questioning his reasons for going to the Black Hills, and he'd told her only that he could always pick up some easy money at the gambling tables, that he wouldn't have to go at all if her husband would pay honest wages. But what brought him here were the holdups, the occasional killing. Hell, it was a lifestyle he enjoyed. Things were changing though, what with the army bringing in more troops, the law in Deadwood and other towns hereabouts getting tough, not to count this talk of organizing a vigilante committee. Once they robbed the bullion train, this would be his last ride down the outlaw trail. He'd always had a hankering to head down to New Orleans again, there to open his own saloon. After Casandra, life would be kind of dull, but he'd survive.

"According to my informant the gold will be going out early Friday morning."

"Well, this is Tuesday. Tomorrow morning, early, we'll head over and scout out Hat Creek Station. Any mention of the army sending some troops as escort?"

"Not to my recollection," said Pickett, and Winger agreed with this.

Killane was the first to leave, and he wandered downtown. He found the other hands at the Silver Star saloon. He told them of meeting with Nate Winger, the bare bones of the plans for the holdup. But he kept to himself the name of Henry Banner. Somehow he had to get Banner headed west into Wyoming. On reflection, it rankled him somewhat that he'd obeyed Casandra's orders to gun down the man; generally he got paid handsomely for such work. He reckoned that she owned him something."

"It's time to pass the collection plate," he told himself.

14

Fifteen minutes after Long Henry had gone into the Lobby saloon he'd gotten into a poker game. It was a dollar limit game, which wasn't to his liking, but he kept on playing just to pass the time. To his left and around the table sat two miners, then a local businessman, J. H. Adams, he called himself, the owner of a grocery store, and finally, a corporal on leave from Fort Meade. The stripes on the lower left sleeve indicated that the corporal had twelve years of service, and like a veteran, he played cautiously, but not grudgingly when he lost a pot. The miners played like, well, miners, thought Long Henry, wanting to raise when they didn't have too much showing, pausing to banter with one another or others at the table, then tossing down a drink and laughing, while the merchant, Adams, kept his cards folded carefully in his hands, not saying too much, pursing his lips when someone else raised, and fitting the pattern, Long Henry figured, of someone who'd only put eleven ounces in a pound bag of flour or sugar.

Within an hour Long Henry was about thirty dollars ahead. Losing most of this money had been the merchant, who kept throwing irritated glances at the piano, the tinny sound of it getting to some others too because one of the keys seemed to be broken, and whenever the pianist, a runt of an Irishman wearing a derby and spats, touched that key the song he was playing at the moment seemed to lose some of its meaning. The merchant said sourly, "Somebody ought to do something about that piano."

The corporal reached to throw a chip onto the pile. "I've heard worse."

"Well, merchant," said one of the miners, "You folding or what?"

"Count me out." Picking up the few chips he had left, the merchant shoved his chair away and rose to leave the saloon.

Smiles broke out around the table, and after calling the last raise, Long Henry found that his three tens were no match for the corporal's heart flush. The sound of the piano, the merchant's departure from the game, had distracted him, but still there was the feeling of his being watched. Without turning his head he studied those in the range of his vision, the few idlers standing around watching the gambling tables, others who were moving into another room where a Keno game was in progress, the customers lining the bar. He played a few more hands, then cashed in his chips and went outside and upstreet in search of his partner.

When Long Henry was past the Overland Hotel, he veered toward a display window and drew up there to see if he was being followed. His attention was drawn to a man idling in front of the hotel, and he started that way, but checked himself when a woman came out of the hotel and moved off with the man he'd been watching. "You're getting jumpy," he murmured.

He came across Deacon O'Shay in the Custer House saloon. At O'Shay's beckoning nod, he made his way through the tables, and to his surprise heard O'Shay introduce him as Matt Bennett, a wealthy Texas rancher up here to have a go at a good time.

"Mr. Bennett, this is J.P. Riley, a gold speculator out of Chicago, I believe."

"That's right," said the man, and shaking Long Henry's hand. "Mr. O'Shay, here, was kind enough to tell me about a no-limit poker game which'll be held at the Merchant's Hotel."

"Now, here's someone special," said O'Shay, and smiling at an older woman seated at the table. "Matt, this is Poker Alice Tubbs."

"Grab a chair, Mr. Bennett," said Poker Alice around the cigar wedged into one corner of her mouth. "Around here we don't stand much on formalities." Poker Alice had a square face and shrewd eyes, and she wore no makeup. Her graying hair was cut short and held in place by a knot at the back of her head.

"Poker Alice runs one of the finest houses of pleasure in Sturgis," went on O'Shay.

"Ma'am," Long Henry said pleasantly. Settling onto a chair, his eyes met O'Shay's; a silent question.

"Mr. Riley, I'd be pleased if you'd escort Poker Alice over to the hotel," said O'Shay. "We'll be along presently."

When they were alone, Long Henry said, "Mr. Bennett, huh?"

"Sooner or later, my friend, we'll go our separate ways. Me, well, this traveling is beginning to wear me down. Kind of hankering to find a nice place to settle in . . . become a pillar of the community. You're getting restless too, Henry. Oh, I know she's out west someplace. But what if you never find her? Or that gunslinger? Getting your voice back, Henry, is a good sign. Now, I don't know your reasons for not wanting to talk much. But tonight I reckon you'll have to do your own palavering in this game."

"No-limit?"

"Tonight the sky's the limit. Some big money boys will be in the game. Working together, we can probably clean up."

"Okay, boss, we'll play it your way."

O'Shay pulled out his pocket watch. "Another hour before the game starts."

"That woman, who is she?"

Swinging his eyes to the staircase, O'Shay looked at a woman moving regally down the steps. The black silky gown showed her figure to good advantage, with lamplight touching the burnished head of chestnut hair. The face was oval, and showing some tan on the sunken cheekbones and forehead, while her large eyes looked directly but not boldly at those she passed as she came through the tables. His partner had never been a woman chaser, but from the look on Long Henry's face, O'Shay knew that he was taken with the woman. Rising, O'Shay called out, "Molly Corcoran, a pleasure seeing you again."

"Why, Deacon?" She moved over and threw her arms around O'Shay. "One of the honest ones."

"Still playing it aboveboard, Molly."

". . . and . . . who is this?" She gazed up into Long Henry's eyes, a flush darkening her flawless skin, a message passing between them.

"My partner, Henry Banner, out of Texas."

At first, it was as if Casandra had stood up there, and close like this, there was a faint resemblance. But he was more disturbed by Molly Corcoran's presence than he dared to admit. During the years of his wanderings he hadn't gotten involved with any women, steeled by the deep pain within. This one had no guile, he sensed, yet there was a toughness about Molly Corcoran that one felt rather than saw, and she was beautiful in her own way.

"A pleasure meeting you, Miss Corcoran."

"Molly owns this place," said O'Shay. "Care to join us for a drink?"

"I'd like that, Deacon. But only if I'm buying."

When they were settled around the table, Long Henry let his partner do most of the talking, though he opened up at times. The hour passed too quickly for him, and then they were standing to leave, with Long Henry promising to come back and see Molly Corcoran. Outside, and walking with O'Shay over to the Merchant's Hotel, Long Henry realized that he'd forgotten about being followed, remembering only when they were entering the lobby.

Deacon O'Shay went ahead along a corridor and into a billiard room, with the door being closed again by one of the housemen. Two of those who would participate in the poker game were playing billiards, and O'Shay and Long Henry went to where Poker Alice Tubbs was seated at an ornately-carved gambling table, and talking to the gold speculator from Chicago and two other men. Dark-stained wood covered the walls, red drapes were closed over the windows, and the tile on the floor had intricate patterns in it. There were two housemen, one acting as bartender and standing behind a corner bar, the man who'd opened the door moving back to a long table on which there were platters of food, poker chips in holders and spare decks of cards. Games like these, Long Henry knew, could go on for several hours or days, and with a lot of money changing hands.

As his custom was, Long Henry studied those who'd be in the game. Riley, the gold speculator, had the look of a man who knew his way around town, but being he was employed by someone else, probably wouldn't have the funds for a long poker run, and would play more cautiously than the others. Riley looked crisp and lean in the eastern-style suit, and his blond hair was parted in the middle. The woman, Poker Alice, was here because she enjoyed the game; she'd be a tough one to beat out. Her introduction of the others at the table, Edward Trimble, the manager of the Homestake Gold Mine located nearby, and a banker from Sturgis, O.T. Watkins, revealed to Long Henry that they had the money to back up their play.

The houseman who was acting as barkeep spoke. "Since everyone's here, I suggest that the game commence."

The two men who'd been playing billiards laid their cues down and came over to find places at the table. One of them stated that he was John Fairwell, an employee of a local bank, the other man saying he ranched south of the Black Hills, that his name was Ash Leonard. The bank employee, to Long Henry's way of thinking, had gone to seed some. Fairwell was overweight, the suit he wore was rumpled, the eyes in the round face evasive and showing a false confidence. On the other hand, Ash Leonard's craggy face revealed little of what the man was thinking, and he was solid through the chest and arms. Beside Poker Alice and the men with the big money, Trimble and Watkins, Ash Leonard was the one to watch.

The first hour passed quickly, as did the second and third, and during this time Long Henry found that his preliminary judgment of those in the game had proven correct. Except for the overhead lamp, the large room was cloaked in darkness, the table with the food on it and the corner bar close enough to be seen, and John Fairwell's signals for the houseman to fetch him another drink coming more often. The man had been losing heavily, and during the course of the game he'd opened up about himself, bragging that he was the head teller at the Merchants National Bank. By Long Henry's estimate Fairwell had lost a lot more than he could ever earn as a bank employee, and if the other players, with the exception of Deacon O'Shay, were aware of this, it seemed they were just happy to help relieve Fairwell of what money he still had.

Whenever Deacon O'Shay was betting heavily on a hand, Long Henry would quietly fold, not wanting to buck his partner. Then, he'd draw on his cigarette and closely watch the other players, seeing how they called, and too, noticing the little telltale signs of facial expression or body movement. At the five hour mark play was halted, and the players went to freshen up, either eating or having a drink or two, or going to the bathroom. The gold speculator, Riley, had been forced

117

to buy more chips to replenish those he'd lost, and the banker from Sturgis wasn't too far behind. O'Shay had the most chips at the table, with the manager of the Homestake Gold Mine trailing behind, and right up there too was Ash Leonard.

"Tell me, Texas," said Ash Leonard, "how's the ranching business?"

"Tough, like everything else."

"Been watching you play," went on Leonard. "You seem preoccupied."

"Poker isn't everything."

"Reckon there are a hell of a lot of other things to worry a man, that's for sure."

Long Henry helped himself to a ham and cheese sandwich, a cup of coffee, and knowing that the rancher had been right, that he was more preoccupied with thoughts of Molly Corcoran, along with that nagging feeling that he'd soon meet someone out of the past. He'd been winning, but not as much as he was capable of, and at the moment this game of poker didn't seem the most important thing in the world.

When the game resumed, Long Henry blocked from his mind any distracting thoughts. He began winning heavily. By now, Fairwell was drunk, dropping his chips or cards and swearing, and around five in the morning he lurched away from the table, having lost all of his money. "Damn!" he cried out, as one of the housemen let him out of the billiard room.

Soon after that, the gold speculator quit playing too, and though he'd lost heavily, left with a cheerful smile. By his calculations, Long Henry was about seven thousand winners, and across the table, the stack of chips before Deacon O'Shay was of considerable size, with the rancher, Ash Leonard having a lot of chips left too. The others, Poker Alice, Trimble, Watkins, had lost heavily, but didn't seem too concerned about this. The raises were higher now, fifty to a hundred dollars, and though Long Henry was as tired as the others, he kept a tight rein on his emotions and cards. It was the ebb and flow of games like this that he enjoyed, for by now he could pretty well tell, by the lay of the cards spread out before the players on the green felt cloth, who had the high hand. And even though he was well ahead in the game, his instincts as a professional gambler kept him from making that reckless raise or bucking another hand that seemed to be a sure winner.

Around seven o'clock, and with light seeping through the drawn curtains, the banker from Sturgis called it quits, followed a half-hour later by Trimble, looking tired and worried now, and departing quietly.

Said Poker Alice: "Well, gents"—cigar smoke billowed past her seamed face—"if I don't win this hand I'm cleaned out. But, what the hell, it's been enjoyable." She slid her remaining chips into those piled in the center of the table. "Gimme two cards."

Deacon O'Shay discarded one card, was dealt another, which he slipped in with those he held without looking at what he'd been given, his eyes going to the others still holding cards. "I'll call you."

"Three kings, gents," said Poker Alice, and laying her cards faceup on the table.

With the exception of O'Shay, the others threw in their cards, and he murmured softly, "I was drawing to an inside straight . . . which goes against my gambling instincts." He studied his cards, and smiled to ease the sight of his placing the winning hand on the table. "Sorry to do that, Poker Alice."

"Nothing to be sorry about, Deacon." Wearily, she rose, adding, "You gents better head over to Sturgis and see my girls. After tonight, I could sure use the money." Trailing cigar smoke, Poker Alice left the room.

Ash Leonard glanced at the few chips left in front of him. "I've lost considerable, I reckon. Let's see, got about three hundred in chips. So deal the pasteboards, Mr. O'Shay."

Upon picking up the cards dealt to him, Long Henry discovered that he had the makings of a heart flush. And glancing over at O'Shay, saw the man's customary poker face. But in Ash Leonard's eyes there was a gleam of hope, and he drawled, "I'm betting everything here. One card." Then he shoved the rest of the chips into the pot.

Discarding a single card, Long Henry received another to take its place, to find that he hadn't hit his heart flush, but he kept his hand, and watched as O'Shay discarded two cards, picked up those he'd just dealt himself without checking to see what he had. Ash Leonard, as observed by Long Henry, seemed to have perked up considerably over the hand he held now. Leonard asked the houseman to bring him another shot of whiskey, and one of them imported Cuban cigars too.

"And fetch me a pencil and paper," he said. When this was brought, the rancher looked at the other players. "My ranch against your chips, gentlemen."

From the tone of the rancher's voice, Long Henry knew that Leonard had hit big, and he swung his eyes over to O'Shay, read instantly the look of calm assurance, knew that his partner was also holding some good cards.

Fastening a tired smile, Long Henry discarded his hand. "Too rich for my blood, Ash. You two fight it out."

Ash Leonard scribbled on the piece of paper. "I'm deeding my ranch to the winner of this here game, Mr. O'Shay, that is, if you see fit to call my last raise?"

"Well, Mr. Leonard," came back O'Shay, "by my estimate I've got pretty close to thirty thousand dollars here. Your ranch worth that much?"

"That, and more. Got a large herd, damned near a thousand head of prime steers, and fifteen thousand acres for them to graze on. But I don't figure on losing this here game, Mr. O'Shay." He drew confidently on the cigar.

"Neither do I," and saying that, Deacon O'Shay slid the stacks of chips into the pile. "I've called you, sir."

Downing the whiskey in the shot glass, Ash Leonard sighed deeply, savoring this moment. "This is one of the sweetest hands I've ever been dealt." One by one the rancher placed a card faceup on the table, the six, seven, eight of spades. Pausing, he smiled broadly. "You want to see the rest of them, Mr. O'Shay?"

"It would be appreciated."

But Long Henry shoved away from the table, knowing that Ash Leonard had hit a straight flush, possibly the highest hand in poker, and almost unbeatable. This was the way of gambling, he knew, and for certain lady luck hadn't given his partner anything close to beating what the rancher held. Then, Ash Leonard laid down the nine and ten of spades.

"Well, Mr. O'Shay," he boomed out, "beat that straight flush!"

It wasn't Deacon O'Shay's way to humiliate a man, especially one of Ash Leonard's caliber, and the assured glance he cast over at Long Henry told his partner that Deacon O'Shay had hit big too. Stretching out an arm, he placed his cards besides those of the rancher's, said quietly, "There they are, sir."

Through disbelieving eyes Ash Leonard stared at the solid mass of red cards placed there by his opponent. He seemed to sag in his chair, the craggy face a mass of confusion, and he mumbled, "A straight flush, too?"

"But a little higher than yours, I'm afraid."

"Reckon so, Mr. O'Shay, reckon so." He heaved himself up from the chair. "Guess I'll mosey along."

"Ash, would you be so kind as to take this money."

"A thousand dollars? That's a heap of money."

Deacon O'Shay nodded. "I'd like you to stay on at the ranch, Mr. Leonard, until I can get down there. Which could be some time."

"Well, got no other place to go."

When the rancher had left, Long Henry said, "That was decent of you, partner."

"The man never expected to lose his ranch. Henry, you know I'm no rancher." He picked up the piece of paper signed by Ash Leonard. "The place is yours if you want it."

"You always did know where a man's weak spot was, Deacon. But I'll have to think on it."

"Do that. Right about now steak and eggs sounds good. I'm buying."

"Considering you won most of the money in this

here game, I'll take you up on it."

O'Shay laughed softly. "You don't realize it, my friend, but for a man who doesn't want to let on he can talk, you're doing a lot of it."

"Guess some habits can be broken after all."

15

Long Henry slept through the day and came awake sometime after sundown. His first remembrance was of the poker game, and its outcome. There would be no gambling for awhile, just the need to unburden himself from the thought of it. He gambled to make a living, while for O'Shay it was a way of life. The offer of the ranch was mighty tempting. But growing stronger in him was the desire to head out for St. Louis. Still, here in this gold mining haven there would be more big games.

"Molly Corcoran," he murmured, and trying to frame a picture of her in his mind. The owner of a saloon met plenty of men, but somehow Molly didn't look like the type of woman who'd throw herself at any man. Climbing out of bed, he headed for the bathroom, having it in mind to go over to her saloon. He needed the companionship of someone other than his partner, and if he asked, she just might consider going out for supper with him.

After placing most of the money he'd won in a money belt, he secured it around his waist, and then finished dressing. Upon reaching the street, Long

Henry saw that a few stores were still open, and a cursory look around told him that no strangers were lurking about. For some reason, the bank teller, John Fairwell, kept edging into his thoughts. Had to be stealing from the bank where he worked, and with that thought, Long Henry moved upstreet until he came to a clothing store and went inside. The new Stetson he purchased he put on in place of his old one, and after buying other items of clothing, asked that they be delivered to the Merchant's Hotel.

When Long Henry went into the Custer House Saloon, he was disappointed to find that Molly Corcoran wasn't around, and he stepped up to the bar. He ordered a drink while looking around at the gambling action taking place. Much to his surprise the barkeep brought a small envelope along with the beer he'd ordered, saying, "The drink's on the house."

Long Henry pulled out a folded sheet of paper from the envelope. "Mr. Banner," it went, "I would enjoy your presence at my house for supper. Molly C." There were instructions on how to get there.

As Molly Corcoran's instructions had detailed, it was the small house on the north side of Broadway Street, and there was the white picket fence with the lilac bushes strung out along it, their aromatic scent following Long Henry as he passed through the gate and went up the walkway. Light came through the open doorway, and clambering onto the porch, he knocked lightly at the closed screen door.

"Come in," came her voice.

Removing his hat, he moved inside, to have her tell

him to come on into the kitchen. "Glad you could make it, Mr. Banner."

"Glad to be here."

From the oven she removed a hot dish, and turned to face him, her chestnut hair tumbling to her shoulders, and presenting a different appearance from last night, for Molly had on a sedate gingham dress and a fluffy apron. It had been a long time since Long Henry had found himself in such a situation, and he stood there awkwardly, not certain of what was expected of him. And for want of something to say, he murmured, "Nice place."

"It'll do. I hope you like beef stew."

"One of my favorites." He followed her into the living room, where she set the hot dish on the table and beckoned for him to sit down. During the meal he began to relax as Molly told of how she took over running the saloon when her father passed away.

"It hasn't been easy," she said.

"But you look like you survived. I gather that these are Deacon's old stomping grounds."

"On occasion they are. I was surprised to see he had a partner this time around. Henry, this isn't fair; here you've been letting me do all the talking. Tell me something about yourself?"

And to Long Henry's surprise he found himself opening up to the lovely Molly Corcoran, telling her sketchily of his short term as marshal of Waco, and some of the other details of the shooting, of Casandra. "Maybe she isn't alive, Molly. But I haven't stopped looking."

"She must have been quite a woman, Henry."

"In her own way. Sorry, I didn't mean to unburden myself like that."

"I'm glad you did. Will you be staying long?"

"Don't rightly know, Molly."

"Long enough to go for a walk?"

"What about the dishes?"

Molly laughed and came lightly to her feet. "I'll take care of them later."

They left the house and walked along a street curling toward the canyon rim. She stumbled once on the gravelly surface, and he held out a steadying hand, smiled back when she murmured her thanks. Spread out below were the lights of Deadwood, but up here the scent of fir trees enveloped them, along with an awareness of one another. Moonlight came through branches set to rustling by a gentle breeze.

"I come up here often."

"It's peaceful."

While he gazed down at the lights, Molly studied this tall and lonely man, thinking about what Deacon O'Shay had told her about him. There weren't many eligible men around here, and she rarely went out. Henry Banner was different somehow, he'd suffered much at the hands of another woman. Molly realized that it would be very easy to fall in love with him. She could sense his inner loneliness, see on his face how the years had changed him, and knew that the one thing Henry Banner needed right now was a woman.

Placing a hand on his arm, she said, "I want you to kiss me."

Wordlessly, he drew her close, found her seeking lips, and after a long while she whispered, "Now Texas, I want you to share my bed tonight." Molly Corcoran smiled when she saw the answer glimmering in his eyes. "Come."

At the canyon floor the street they were on joined another, and they went along Broadway toward Molly's house. Suddenly, a man screamed out in pain. "No! Please . . . you gotta believe me!"

The man's voice seemed to be coming from a large frame building just down the street, and Long Henry said, "Wait here." Then he went ahead to the closed doors of a livery stable. The doors were bolted from the inside, and he went around to a side wall and peered in through an open window. No light showed in the building, but he could make out the dim forms of horses tethered in stalls. He heard the unmistakable thud of a fist striking flesh, followed by a gasp of pain.

"I swear, Winger, you're the only one I've told about this."

"Fairwell, you've been dealing double!"

"No . . . I swear . . ."

It was the bank clerk, realized Long Henry.

"Don't deny it, Fairwell," came a third voice. "The question is, who else have you told about this besides Winger and me?"

Fairwell broke, began crying, and outside Long Henry tensed, wanting the men who'd just spoken to do so again. And tracking that voice down the backtrail of time to when he'd been marshal of Waco, determining that it could be an outlaw he'd sent to prison.

"Bank clerk," the third man said, "you're a regular canary."

"Please . . . no . . ." Fairwell screamed in agony.

Now to Long Henry's disbelief came the sound of laughter such as he'd heard down in Waco on the night he'd been shot from ambush. Navajo Killane was in there! Spinning away from the window, he pulled out his weapon and ran back along the wall to stumble against an untidy pile of crates and debris, and to have a crate clatter noisily to the ground.

"Let's vamoose!" someone shouted.

Recovering his balance, Long Henry spun around the back corner of the building. There was nobody in sight, and he moved ahead to the back door swinging back from where it had been flung open. He crouched inside, found that the man who'd attacked the bank clerk was gone, but Fairwell lay there not moving. He went to the man, knelt down, and felt for a pulse.

"Murdered," he murmured, and coming erect. And by Navajo Killane. If Killane was here, Casandra couldn't be far away. After seven long years he'd finally found the gunslinger, mixed up in some criminal activity, and killing again.

"Don't move, Banner!"

Stiffening, Long Henry resisted the urge to turn and fire at the man behind him. He braced himself to receive a slug, but to his surprise the man said, "If you want Killane, you'd best head for Cheyenne!"

"But Killane's here?" The sound of the man's retreating footsteps was the only answer Long Henry received. This was a puzzling turn of events. Now he keened his ears to the night sounds of Deadwood, and knew that what had happened here had gone unnoticed. As a gambler, he didn't want to get mixed up in this. The body would be discovered when the stable opened in the morning, and he left the livery stable.

"What happened?"

"Someone got himself killed."

"Shouldn't we tell the marshal—"

"Look, Molly, I'm new in town, and a gambler. If I reported this, your marshal most likely wouldn't believe that I didn't have a hand in it. Come morning, Fairwell's body will be found."

"John Fairwell?"

"The man is mixed up in something, Molly. He lost pretty heavily in our poker game last night. More than he could earn as a bank clerk. Have you heard of a man called Winger?"

"Could be Nate Winger. Folks around here think Winger's mixed up with an outlaw gang. Why do you ask?"

He opened the gate, and she passed ahead of him down the front walkway. "Winger seems to be one of those involved in the killing."

"Are you hiding something from me?"

"Look, Molly," he said, as they moved onto the porch, "I'll be leaving town."

"Not tonight, I hope?"

"It's something I've got to do."

"It has to do with her, doesn't it?"

"Yes, it does, Molly. Tell the marshal what I've told

you. That I'll come back here to testify as to what I heard."

"Where are you heading, Henry?"

"West." He gathered her in his arms, seeing the promise of what she'd offered him shining in her eyes. They kissed, and after a long while a reluctant Long Henry hurried away.

16

"I'll hear you out, Major Culley, but I'm not going to ship the gold."

The speaker was Ezra Winslow, the owner of Deadwood's Merchants National Bank.

Major Tom Culley, sandy-haired, energetic, paced to a window in the banker's spacious office. Upon learning that John Fairwell had been killed, Culley had hurried up from Fort Meade. At the moment he was wearing civilian clothes, and he said briskly, "Your head teller knew about the gold shipment. Fact. He'd tipped off the Winger bunch about this, a fact which can work in our favor, Mr. Winslow, if you'll change your mind about not shipping the gold bullion."

"It's too risky now."

"If you don't send out those wagons, sir, the problem will still exist."

"I don't understand."

"For about six months now I've been on detached duty, as have others under my command. Our objective is to wipe out these outlaw gangs. One of my men has secured the confidence of Nate Winger. As a matter of fact, Sergeant Lew Pickett was given a bad-conduct discharge, drummed out of the army for selling guns to undesirables. In reality, Pickett is working undercover for me. He knows the intentions of the Winger gang, when they plan to hit your wagon train, Mr. Winslow."

"All this means is that some of my men can get killed."

"There is that risk," agreed Major Culley.

"Which I cannot take at this point in time."

"Hear me out, sir. Pickett has in his possession a Gatling gun. I can assure you that Pickett will render it inoperable before it can be used against your men. And, sir, I have taken the liberty of sending two cavalry units on ahead into the Black Hills. We know your time of departure from Deadwood, we know your route of travel . . ."

"As do the outlaws, I'm afraid."

"Instead of shipping any gold tomorrow morning, load your wagons with rocks instead. My troopers will keep Hat Creek Station under surveillance. Then, we'll be able to wipe out Winger's gang."

"I don't know . . ."

"Your head teller informed Winger that you hadn't requested any soldiers as escort. Consider the element of surprise, the appearance of the cavalry, and the fact, sir, that the Gatling gun won't enter into it."

"Major Culley, you should have been a recruiting officer. Very well, my wagon train will leave as scheduled."

"Now, Mr. Winslow, here's what I want you to do."

* * *

There wasn't much to the place where Navajo Killane and his men had camped, the crumbling remains of a log cabin and pole corral, but the trees lining the creek gave them shelter and water, and the glow of the campfire couldn't be seen for more than fifty yards. Though the sky was lightening some, it was still hard to distinguish ground objects. The five men with Killane either hung close to the fire or moved about to drive away the morning chill. Pine cones were strewn under the firs, the scent of the trees coming strong. The horses were stirring, moving about at the ends of picket ropes, and with some of them nibbling at what grass there was under the trees.

In a little while Navajo Killane would have more money than he'd ever seen in his life, and he felt good about that idea, bantering with the others seated around the fire. They were waiting for Winger and his men to show.

"How come Talbot and Petrie aren't here?"

"They'll be along," Killane assured the others.

"Me, I figure on taking my share and heading out to San Francisco. Got a hankering to smell that ocean air again. Might even ship out to sea for a spell."

One of the hands approached the campfire. "Riders coming in."

Nodding, Killane mumbled, "Pass that bottle over here. Damn, I feel good."

Out of the dimness several riders appeared, to dismount and ground hitch their horses. Nate Winger came in first, walking awkwardly in his cowboy boots and hitching to get his belt up over his protruding belly. "Any coffee left?" A cup was tossed to him, and he reached for the blackened pot hanging over the flames, poured the cup full. By Killane's count, fifteen more men settled down nearby, and to the newcomers Killane's men passed around whiskey bottles.

"All right," Killane began, "Winger and me, and Pickett, there, scouted out the lay of the land around Hat Creek Station. The stagecoach road runs through some hills until it cuts through this narrows about a mile east of the station. I want some of your men, Winger, to block off the west end of the narrows, the others will be on the rocks above, as will my men. Once Pickett starts hitting them with that Gatling gun"—he took a long drink of whiskey—"I reckon they'll be too busy trying to survive than return our fire. We've got extra pack horses for the gold. Any questions?"

"Which way you planning on heading after this is over?" Winger asked.

"Like I told you before, Nate, which way you hightail it is pretty much up to you and your men."

"You mean everyone's on their own."

"Best that way," said Killane. "We bunch up afterwards, we'll leave too big a trail. Best way is to break up in to twos or threes and head every which way."

"I agree," said Winger. Sipping at the coffee, he regarded Killane across the fire. "By now they've found that bank teller. Think they'll still be coming?"

Killane grinned. "We'll sure as hell find out. Clearing some. About time to head out. Mount up."

* * *

135

While trees were felled and dragged across the road to block the western end of the narrows, the rest of the outlaws divided into two groups, one party led by Nate Winger taking up position on the rimrocks, the other under Killane settling behind rocks to the north. From his vantage point, Killane could see the road wending down from the hills to the east. The sun had cleared the horizon, and the glare of it caused him to squint some as he checked the action of his Remington before bringing the rifle to his right shoulder and sighting in at the narrow portion of road snaking through the narrows below. One of the hands began playing softly on a harmonica to pass the time. Killane had a clear view of Winger and his men opposite, and not liking the way they were moving about and exposing themselves.

"Greenhorns," he muttered disdainfully, and scowled when sunlight reflected off their rifles. "It'll be a miracle if we pull this off."

"Lucky we're not setting an ambush for the Sioux; those Injuns would turn the tables on us."

Behind Killane and his men and lower on the slope, their mounts pulled against the picket line, and turned to cock their ears to the north and the hills there. "I don't like it."

"Probably Winger's men got them stirred up," retorted Killane. "Or it could be a black bear."

"Reckon that's it," agreed the hand.

As the day warmed, mist and shadows left the low places. A hawk flew in indolent circles overhead, then swung away when it spotted the men lurking along the rimrock. Further to the west and on the same side of the narrows as Winger's men, the cashiered soldier, Pickett, had placed his Gatling gun. He was the only man with field glasses, and could be seen by Killane using them to scan the approaches from the east. Killane was getting impatient, his blood stirred by the whiskey he'd drunk. By his reckoning it was after nine.

"Be a shame that gold train didn't show," said Davis, one of the hands.

"Yeah," Killane snarled, swatting at a gnat buzzing around his face. Then he came alert when Pickett signalled the arrival of the gold train by pumping an arm up and down several times, and Killane exclaimed, "Get ready!"

Earlier, Killane had instructed everyone not to fire until the gold train was well into the narrows, and thinking that Winger's men would probably panic and open up before that. With that Gatling gun, he saw no need for the other bunch. But within a few minutes Winger and his men would be cut to ribbons by Pickett, and Killane smiled at the thought. He wasn't about to share this gold with scum like that.

The first outriders crested a rise and came at a canter along the stagecoach road. Wagons appeared, high-sided and covered with hoop-supported canvas tarp, each one with a driver and another riding shotgun. Five wagons; twelve outriders. And coming in steadily. A cloud shadow passed overhead as the wagons entered the narrows, the men below scanning the rimrocks.

Killane could feel the pleasure at what was to come building, the tension at his temples, that sensuous feeling at his groin. He sighted in on one of the front riders, a distance of less than a hundred yards, and for the gunslinger an easy shot. As his finger applied pressure to the trigger, the outriders suddenly flung themselves out of their saddles coincident with the blaring of bugles coming from the north and again southward. Twisting around, Killane stared in disbelief at cavalryman spread out in a scrimmage line at the base of the slope behind him. A bullet chipped the rock close to his head, and Killane swung around and began returning the fire of those with the gold train.

"We've been doublecrossed!" someone shouted.

A survivor's instinct brought Navajo Killane away from the rimrock and toward a jumble of rocks further down the slope, where he picked his way through the rocks. Coming behind him were two other cowhands. Below, the troopers came on steadily, urging their mounts around huge boulders and up the tree-speckled slope. Killane's only thought was to reach the horses, visible to him in a little rocky cul-de-sac. When he reached a cleared space, Killane dropped to one knee. The others reached him, held up.

"They haven't spotted our horses yet!"

"Then what are we waiting for?"

"Davis, circle over that way. We bunch up, those bluebellies are sure to spot us. And, Ripken, make tracks over there."

The others slipped to either side and Killane worked his way from tree to tree. He held his fire. Now the troopers began returning the fire of Davis, Ripkin. Through narrowed eyes Killane pondered and said angrily, "The Gatling gun? . . . It ain't being fired? That damn Pickett pulled this doublecross!"

Emerging from behind a fir, Killane felt a bullet brush his foot, and he fired back at three troopers about seventy yards below where the horses were picketed, the horses still hidden from these men but tugging wildly at the picket line and rearing in alarm. Killane scored a hit, laughed mirthlessly, the sun glinting off his gold-studded teeth.

When Killane reached the pocket of rocks where the horses were picketed, Davis arrived also, but blood stained the man's left shoulder. They closed on the surging horses, each picking out a mount. Killane's horse lashed out with flailing forehoofs, its eyes rolling crazily in their sockets, and he cursed at it before scrambling into the saddle, where he pulled out his knife and cut the picket line.

"Head 'em at those bastards!" he yelled, as the freed horses cut around the rocks and took the easier route downhill; one of the freed horses lost its footing and fell awkwardly, sprang up again to spurt after the other horses leaving a trail of dust and Killane and the other cowhand behind.

Levering another shell into the breech of his rifle, Killane snapped a quick shot at Davis riding slightly ahead, and smiled when Davis snapped upright in shock before spilling out of the saddle. Then Killane was in the wake of confused dust left by the horses, the few troopers he encountered just picking themselves up from where they'd avoided the stampeding horses. Still, a few slugs followed Killane's flight.

The gunslinger reached the base of the slope, let his horse have its head in a vain attempt to catch up with the other horses, then he tugged back on the reins and went on at a lope across a meadow spangled with flowers and to the crest of another hill, where he stopped to stare back at the rimrock above the stage-coach road. The sound of gunfire came sharply to him.

"Damn that Pickett!" he mumbled bitterly. There went any hopes of heading down to New Orleans. Most of this was Winger's fault, him and them damned petty thieves he called a gang. Half a million in gold bullion that could'a been his.

"No sense looking up a dead horse's ass now," he muttered.

From a shirt pocket he fished out a pouch of Perique, a rich-flavored tobacco produced in Louisiana. As he rode, he fashioned a cigarette, while letting his mind settle down. Gunning down Davis had been a reflexive action, a means of seeing that there was one less to testify against him. Ripkin, the other hands, hell's bells, this hadn't been no Sunday school class. No question in Killane's mind that these men would hang, that is, if they weren't dead already. And then there was Winger and his mangy bunch, which was where his worry was concentrated now. Those bastards would spill everything for two fingers of rotgut. Dragging smoke into his lungs, Killane's thoughts turned to Casandra McClintock.

"Henry Banner," he murmured. Some of the worry left his eyes. It was a stroke of luck his spotting Banner back at Deadwood. If everything went according to plan, Banner should be on his way to Cheyenne by now, with Talbot and Petrie bringing up the man's backtrail. This had to go right, because he was growing weary of trying to deal with Casandra. She wasn't the woman she'd been down in New Orleans. And he'd have to make his move right away, what with Jason McClintock being sick and all.

"Yup, time to pass that collection plate."

It was a long way to Big Horn country, but savagely Navajo Killane dug his roweled spurs into the flanks of his horse, setting it to galloping. Along the way, he reckoned, he'd come across a ranch or two, maybe a town, where there were fresh horses and women.

17

To the west clouds were building over the plains of Territorial Wyoming, cliff-edged hammerheads that jostled one another, thundering their displeasure when one got too close, while a wall of rain stretched from their black bellies toward the ground. Overhead, sunlight broke through rifts in the clouds, struck the two riders, rippled golden through prairie grass bending with the freshening wind. Now they brought their horses along a patch of dry land lying between a marshy area where mud hens and mallards were floating in open stretches of water, and where red-wing blackbirds were bobbing on reeds and twanging.

The stiffening wind lashed around the brim of Long Henry's hat as he urged his grulla up a slope, and with Deacon O'Shay following. They drew up together at the edge of a bluff overlooking the south fork of the Cheyenne River and studied the lay of the land beyond.

"Another trail herd," said O'Shay, as he nodded toward a plume of dust to the southwest.

The herd came on toward the river, the sun slid tiredly toward the western horizon, and now a flicker of displeasure revealed itself in Long Henry's eyes when he could distinguish long-horned southern cattle. "From Texas," he muttered. Then his eyes raised a few degrees to the Laramies enshrouded in purplish haze.

"Could use some hot chow," stated O'Shay. "Figure those Texans will be making camp soon."

The last thing Long Henry wanted at the moment was to palaver with a bunch of Texans. He was certain to be recognized, and they'd bring back memories of Casandra. Hanging from a chain encircling his neck was a locket containing her picture. He felt the weight of it now, the touch of it seeming to sear his flesh, and when he looked at her picture the pain that tore at his heart was worse than the occasional spasm that gripped his throat. Besides, a couple of riders had been on their backtrail ever since they'd left Deadwood. And would he actually come across the gunslinger, Killane, in Cheyenne? They could be riding into another ambush. Wheeling the grulla around, and without waiting for his partner, Long Henry rode southward along the bluff.

About a mile south of where they'd seen the trail herd, Long Henry led the way down a break in the rock-strewn slope and through thick brush growing along the river basin. At the river's edge they came across a fallen cottonwood forming an eddying barrier against the brackish waters.

They'd fallen into the routine of O'Shay fashioning the campfire and a meal from the food in their saddlebags while Long Henry tended to the horses. It was closing on sundown by the time O'Shay had the fire going, a pot of coffee hanging over it, their bedrolls spread out nearby. Filling two cups, he brought them along the loamy bank and into a small grove of willow trees where Long Henry had tied the horses. The horses were still saddled, and with both of their rifles close to where they settled down.

"Gonna storm," muttered O'Shay. He handed Long Henry one of the cups.

After he passed O'Shay some beef jerky and hardtack, Long Henry sipped at the coffee, and over the rim of the cup, let his eyes drift to the hammerheads showing reddish hues as the sun sank beneath the horizon, the distant rumble of thunder breaking the silence. Shadows were spreading along the riverside, darkening the brush, and from a nearer distance came the faint lowing of the herd.

"Hated to pull out of Deadwood."

Long Henry smiled. "You didn't have to come."

"Guess the notion of riding alone don't appeal to me, partner. Anyway, I went over to the land office, registered that ranch in your name."

"Then I owe you, Deacon."

"We're square. Ranching is like getting your teeth pulled. Or like trying to fill a straight flush. What if this gunslinger ain't in Cheyenne?"

"He'll be there."

"That so?" He cast Long Henry a searching and curious glance.

"Yup," he said firmly, placing the cup aside.

Night closed down upon them, and it began raining, the rain coming at them in long slanting sheets, and they donned their yellow slickers. The campfire began dying down, but its glow still revealed the bedrolls made up to look as though they were sleeping in them. And then the grulla stamped a nervous forehoof at the ground and cocked its ears to some unseen danger. They picked up their rifles, took up new positions under the trees. It was a strange and eerie night, with the moon coming out from behind clouds for brief spells, bolts of lightning lancing groundward, thunder drumming, the rain sharpening the swampy smell of the river.

Long Henry whistled softly, and Deacon O'Shay nodded that he'd seen the shadowy rider coming in along the bank, and with another ambusher trailing behind. The first rider pulled up short of the campfire and fired at the bedrolls.

"Drop those weapons!" O'Shay cried out, only to have the ambusher respond by firing blindly toward the grove of trees, with the slug striking a rock near O'Shay and ricochetting away. Then he was firing back.

Long Henry slammed two bullets at the closer horseman, and the man fell out of the saddle. He held his fire when the other rider swung around and headed back along the bank to disappear. Easing out of the grove with O'Shay at his side, Long Henry moved cautiously toward the campfire, the glow of it almost gone now, the ambusher crumpled on the far side of it, and closer, he could see the man curled into a ball and clutching at his stomach with both hands. As O'Shay knelt down by the man, Long Henry eased over the fallen tree and grabbed the reins of the ambusher's horse starting to shy away. He tied the reins to a branch, went back to O'Shay.

"Water . . ."

"Hombre, you're gutshot," said O'Shay. "You've been trailing us ever since we left Deadwood."

The knowledge that he was dying shone in the man's eyes. He reached weakly for O'Shay's arm, held on with what grip he had left, as if that would keep the inevitable away. "Wanted your poke . . . gambling man . . ."

"Your greed brought you to this."

"Him . . . was supposed to follow the Texan . . ."

"My pard, here?" said O'Shay.

"Who sent you?" Long Henry asked, as he hunkered down.

A weak grin parted the man's quivering lips. "Find out at . . . Mac . . . Mac . . ." A sort of rattling noise issued from his mouth before life passed from the ambusher.

"Mac?"

"Got to be a man's name?" questioned O'Shay. Rising, he gazed in disgust toward the campfire. "Some damned fool plugged a hole in my coffee pot. And me craving some more java."

The rain was coming down harder now, adding to their discomfort. While Long Henry searched through the ambusher's saddlebags, O'Shay went and brought their horses over to the campfire. Though Long Henry found some food, the usual items in the saddlebags, there were no clues to the man's identity, and all the man had in his pockets were a few silver dollars, a pocket knife, and a tobacco pouch with a wad of paper.

"Even coyotes," complained O'Shay, "can find a place

146

to hole up on a night like this. We'd best make tracks for the trading post at Lance Creek. Want to leave that bushwhacker here?"

"We'll load him on his horse; maybe someone at Lance Creek knows who he is."

Sometime during the rainy night they came across the stagecoach road running from Deadwood to Cheyenne, and clung to it. After a while it stopped raining, with the sky beginning to show a few stars as the cloud cover began dispersing, and there was a paleness to the east. Both men felt easier when the dark shapes of buildings appeared. Rounding a corral where three horses were huddled, they pulled up by a sod-roofed barn, a one-story structure fashioned of logs.

Along the way, Long Henry had tried to put a face to this mysterious man known only as Mac. But there'd been too many towns and faces during the years of his wandering. Swinging to the ground, he removed his Stetson and slapped the rain from it. He was saddle weary, about chilled to the bone. O'Shay went ahead, opened the barn door and led his horse into the manure-odored interior. Long Henry brought the other horses. He left the dead man tied to the saddle, the horse in a stall, then tended to his grulla.

A dog began yowling, and O'Shay said, "Hope that mutt rouses whoever runs this place."

Removing his slicker, Long Henry draped it over a stall wall and moved alongside O'Shay toward the trading post, its bony-sheen log walls catching the glint of new light in the eastern sky. O'Shay hammered at the oaken door, and stopped when light beamed through a front window. The dog appeared, showing its fangs and raised hackles, but kept out of range while barking at the strangers. Finally, the door creaked open a few cautious inches.

"I told you damnable Injuns . . ."

Deacon O'Shay kicked the door inward, marched inside to confront a gaunt-faced man with graying hair curling around his neck. Under the drooping eyes were prominent bags, and he wore red flannels, carried a lantern. O'Shay said, "We rode all night to get here, and that through one hell of a rainstorm. We're coming in." He strode to the pot-bellied stove, removed a lid, and began stuffing hunks of wood into its iron belly. As Long Henry entered, the trader slammed the door shut.

"I have no lodging," the trader said sullenly.

"We want food, hot food, and coffee . . . and be damned quick about it."

"You'll have to wait until sunup for that."

"You deaf, a Russkey, or what?"

"I'm Hans Vettel from Germany."

O'Shay groaned. "One of those." He reached for his revolver. "Well, Hans, let me introduce you to Mr. Colt .45. I suggest you fetch our chow before Mr. Colt .45 loses its temper."

Paling, the trader slipped around a counter and vanished through a back door, and with O'Shay calling after him, "And get dressed; can't stand seeing a grown man running around in his underwear."

Removing his leather coat and flannel shirt, Long Henry found some towels on a wall shelf, used one to dry his face and hair, then his muscular torso. It would be good to get to Cheyenne and a hot bath, but for now this would have to do. He tossed a towel to O'Shay before picking through a pile of woolen shirts and came across one his size, and put it on, the warmth it produced feeling good against his skin. He joined O'Shay by the stove.

"Hope the trader doesn't put arsenic in your grub, Deacon."

"Only way to treat men like him. You gonna ask him if he knows that dead bushwhacker?"

"Later. He might cut and run before we've got a chance to eat."

"Don't look for no feast," said O'Shay, and moving with Long Henry over to a corner table around which several rickety chairs were resting. O'Shay lit the overhead lamp and sat down.

When the trader emerged from a back room bearing two plates, Long Henry was on his second cigarette, while O'Shay was playing a game of solitaire. The trader muttered sourly, "Food costs money. I want to see the color of yours."

"We'll pay if them fixings are any good."

"Now! I want my money now."

"Easy," Long Henry said to his partner. He placed a couple of silver dollars on the table, and the trader set the plates down, scooped up the money with a long, bony hand that had knobby wrists and black hairs showing below the dirty cuff line. He went back to where he'd prepared the food, came back with a pot of coffee.

"Maybe you could help us?"

"It'll cost you to get anything out of this skinflint," cut in O'Shay.

"Any riders come through last night? From the north, that is?"

"Not from that way."

"Know someone called Mac?"

Scowling, the trader mumbled, "No."

Some instinct told Long Henry the man was lying. He took out two more silver dollars, laid them beside his plate. "This man could be riding a horse carrying a Rocking MC brand."

"I tell you, I don't know."

"About as I figured," snorted O'Shay. "Okay, Vettel, just ease yourself onto that chair over there so's I can keep my eye on a skunk like you. Now, you call this leather ham? And these puny little rocks got to be buzzard eggs."

Grinning, Long Henry said, "The coffee is tolerable."

Glowering at the trader, O'Shay picked up his fork and bent to the task at hand. They ate quickly, and after a second cup of coffee, went over and put on their outer garments, and with the trader still hovering over at the corner table. "Outside with you, trader," O'Shay said, as he pulled out his revolver. "We're gonna sashay over to the barn."

"Why?"

"You'll find out when we get there."

They went across the narrow space between the buildings and into the barn, where O'Shay pushed the trader toward the stall in which the dead ambusher was tied to his horse. He grabbed a hunk of hair and raised the man's head, turned the face toward the trader. "Trader, I can tell by the way you've turned a little green around the gills that you know this hombre."

"I . . . he has been here before."

"Then fit a handle to his face—"

"He is the one . . . the one called Talbot."

"Know a gent calling himself Navajo Killane?"

"Killane has been here too. Please, that is all I know. I . . . I am alone out here . . . defenseless against these men . . ."

Scowling, O'Shay took a cigarillo out of his shirt pocket. "You ain't alone, trader . . . 'cause you've got greed for a partner." He wrinkled his nose. "This is sure some stinkhole. Now, Hans Vettel from Germany, I want you to fetch a shovel. Seems you've got to bury this hombre. Back by the manure pile would be a good place for an ambusher. And don't fret now about putting up a cross to mark the grave. I reckon Mr. Talbot, there, is already shoveling coal down in hell." O'Shay went to another stall and reached for his saddle blanket.

Once the trading post fell behind, they followed the angling course of the stagecoach road to the southwest, guided also by the low-crowned Laramies, a mountain range without any distinguishing peaks. They kept their horses to a lope, not wanting them to throw a shoe or otherwise get lamed.

"This seems to be Killane's stomping grounds."

"Appears that way, Deacon."

"It's about a two day ride from this here spot to Cheyenne. Now, Cheyenne, I hear it's got growing pains. Wild and wooly, they say. Got some real card sharks there too."

"Thought you was tired of hearing yourself talk—"

"Which reminds me of back in St. Louie," went on Deacon O'Shay, as though he hadn't heard his partner. "'85, it was. I was dealing faro at the Birdcage and . . ."

18

Casandra McClintock wasn't the same woman she'd been down in Waco. She was more poised, more beautiful, if that was possible, and the eyes that surveyed a wide area of the Powder River flood basin from where she sat with her hands folded over the panel of her saddle had a possessive gleam. McClintock land. Stretching some fifty miles due east, southward, and back around to the north for another fifty to finally end at the foothills of the Big Horn Mountains towering ruggedly behind her. On this bluff she also had a clear view of the ranch site with its many buildings and corrals. She'd fallen in love with the rambling Spanish-style house, and with its lush gardens surrounded by a high stone wall. There, she could completely forget the past, and there, the future was hers.

Jason McClintock's first wife had been Spanish, and though Casandra had kept most of the servants the woman had brought up from Old Mexico, she'd redecorated the interior of the house. To her that house was a touch of civilization in this rugged land, and she had planted some trees alien to this part of the country, as she had been, but she'd adapted well, slowly becoming a force to be reckoned with on the Mac spread.

In a few days they were heading down to Cheyenne, and from there, Denver for a short visit. It would be good to get away from here, and from her dying husband. Ever since the doctors had told her that Jason McClintock had cancer, she'd played the role of the dutiful wife. She would give anything to see Jason's will, but it was highly unlikely that he'd give the ranch to his younger brother, Ox McClintock, a giant of a man, but with the mental development of a child. She had to have the land, for it contained oil deposits, the one thing that would make her a wealthy woman, give her the power she'd always wanted.

Back in West Virginia, her father had worked on oil rigs, earning a meager wage that barely kept food on the table, while those who owned the oil rights became millionaires. Casandra had followed closely the development of Wyoming's Dallas Dome Field. The same rock formations could be found on the Mac spread, and once on a solitary ride she'd come across surface oil. She'd told no one, especially not her husband. Jason McClintock was involved in his cattle operation, hating change, and more than once he'd voiced his displeasure at what the oil companies were doing to ranchland owned by others. Her main reason for going to Cheyenne was to meet with a geologist and sound the man out on coming up here and taking charge of the oil drilling operation she'd start once her husband passed away.

"It's sure pretty, Cassie."

Casandra reined the blooded stallion around and smiled at Ox McClintock, then lifted her eyes to Cloud

154

Peak rising some fourteen thousand feet to touch the darkening sky. Parts of this land would remain with her forever. As for Ox, she'd taken special pains to make him her friend. Eventually he became her bodyguard on her sojourns around the ranch. And if Ox McClintock knew what love was, he reserved it for those times when he was allowed to play with Casandra's son, seven-year old Andrew Jason McClintock.

Ox McClintock was a big, square-built man, stronger than was natural, and always went around wearing a scowl. Mostly, he was the odd job man here at the Mac spread, doing little chores that didn't require too much ability. The other hands used to make Ox the butt of their jokes, joshing about how dumb he was and maybe should be put away someplace. Ox had always been a gentle man, but deep within a rage had been building at his treatment by the other hands. One day he caught one of them pouring molasses into a pair of boots, what Ox called his go-to-town shoes. He proceeded to clamp a bear hug on the hand, wanting to kill what he held. Five other hands piled onto Ox McClintock in an attempt to make him let go, but by that time he'd cracked most of the hand's ribs, fractured one arm. The hand spent five months over at the hospital in Buffalo, never did come back to the Mac spread. Ox McClintock was left alone after that.

"Can I play with Andy when we get back?"

She rode to his side, patted him affectionately on the arm. "Sure . . . and you can have some lemonade too. Want to race back?" Then she spurred away without waiting for him, and along the bluff until she found the narrow track running to the land below.

155

"Hey?" Ox exclaimed. "That's cheating." He turned his large black around and came after her.

Casandra let the stallion have its head, its shod hoofs throwing up clods of bottomland dirt. The outlying buildings flashed by, the blacksmith shop where the smithy was hammering a shoe into shape, and then she drew up sharply in front of a hip-roofed barn, swung to the ground. Ox McClintock rode up and dismounted, his face shining with the joy of the race, and with his little empty eyes gazing at her as he took the reins from her and led the horses into the barn.

She hurried toward the house, passed through an arched gateway adorned with ivy and along a walkway lined with trimmed hedges. In her eyes was the pride of ownership as she gazed at the white stone pillars rising to the second floor balcony, the flight of marble steps leading up to a dark hardwood door that had a stained-glass inset forming the letters MC. The house had a look of permanence, of money, of something planted deep within the hardy earth of territorial Wyoming.

The door swung open and Desmond Parker, the major-domo, stood waiting for Casandra. His skull was shaved, and his prominent features seemed to be carved out of some dark stone. After she crossed the threshold, he closed the door and said, "The doctor is here, Mrs. McClintock."

"How was Jason's day?" She handed him her leather gloves.

"There is some pain. But the new medicine seems to be helping."

"Is everything set for tonight?"

"All will be in readiness. Ah, your husband insists upon mingling with the guests."

"Well, what the hell, it's his party." Casandra smiled inwardly at the glimmer of disapproval in Parker's black eyes. She knew that he was sleeping with one of the Mexican women, but as long as he kept the household under control, she wouldn't tell her husband. She did not trust nor like this black man, avoided him when she could, and when Jason was dead, Desmond Parker would be sent packing. She swept down the gleaming hardwood floor of the long entryway The walls were painted white, the heavy wall and ceiling beams stained a dark brown. As Casandra passed into the main living room and veered toward the curving staircase, a servant appeared, saw the mistress of the house, and melted away again. At the staircase, Casandra turned and looked back at the major-domo.

"Did you discipline that servant girl?"

"I guarantee that Maria will not steal again."

"You know, Parker, we've never gotten along." Casandra forced a smile. "But with Jason under the weather, I'll need you more than ever. I hope I can depend on that."

"I shall do whatever is required of me, Mrs. McClintock."

"If something happens to Jason, I do hope you'll stay on. The job will still be yours if you want it."

"That is most generous of you," he murmured quietly.

Somehow, the lie lifted Casandra's spirits, and she scurried up the stairs and on the second floor found the privacy of her large bedroom. The covered terrace outside her room overlooked the gardens behind the house and the spiny ridge of the Big Horns. Over the wide bed was a canopy and pictures hung from the cream-colored walls. The chest of drawers and vanity had been freighted in from San Francisco. And filling the air was the scent of her perfume. With lingering movements she removed her riding clothes, and naked, cupped her full breasts, wondered if they were beginning to sag. But her figure was good, she knew, the face which gazed back at her from the floor-length mirror that of a mature woman. Reaching to the bed for a silky robe, she slipped into it and padded on bare feet into the bathroom, where her bath had been drawn. As Casandra soaked in the rounded tub, it was a feeling of possessive pride that she thought about her son, Andy. Jason McClintock truly believed that he was the boy's father, and she'd kill the man who said otherwise.

"Men," she said scornfully. How easy it was to deceive them. Three years ago she had sent a trusted agent down to New Orleans. Money had been given to a high ranking police official, with the result that all charges against a prostitute named Casandra Ashbury had been dropped, and with her first husband dead and buried, her future was what she made it. She hadn't told Navajo Killane about the deal that had been struck with the New Orleans police. But the mere recollection of his name, and of his hard body, still stirred the secret parts of her body.

Along with the ambered hues of twilight came many of the guests, invited here by Jason McClintock. They were welcomed by the major-domo and the other servants, shown to their rooms where they could freshen up and change into party clothes. They were expected to stay for a couple of days. And through a bedroom window Casandra could see flames coming from the barbecue pit, where servants were roasting the carcass of a steer. The terrace door was open and balmy night air whispered in, caressing her bare arms and shoulders as she adjusted the black velvety gown. Tonight's party was actually an annual affair in which her husband invited old friends, mostly people from Buffalo and Sheridan, ranchers, cattle buyers and just plain old cowpokes. Jason, she'd found out, was a simple man, not holding to fancy ways, and leaving the welcome mat out for all. This would change, however, when she took over running the Mac spread. There would be no cowpokes with horse shit still clinging to their boots coming into her house.

For appearance's sake Casandra settled a wispy black shawl over her shoulders and turned to the woman hovering near the door. "Carla, make sure my room is tidied up and the lights are out."

Out in the hallway, Casandra went slowly along the long Spanish rug covering the hardwood floor and toward her husband's bedroom, which adjoined hers. She was steeling herself for this visitation. Inhaling deeply, she paused just outside the open door while waiting for the doctor to finish treating Jason McClintock. He was a shell of the man she'd married in Abilene. She smiled at the remembrance of how they'd fled Waco, his insistence that he take her to Abilene, her telling Jason that it would only be a matter of days before the divorce became final, and of Jason, the gallant warrior, wanting to go back and challenge the marshal of Waco to a gun duel, and it was lucky that she'd managed to talk him out of it, because Henry Banner would have shot the rancher's balls off, and then there would have been no persistent courtship, which led to her surrendering to him in an Abilene hotel, or marriage that produced a male child eight months later, and the wildest celebration that the Mac spread or the neighboring ranches and towns had ever seen, and in which Jason McClintock proudly proclaimed the child to be of his own flesh and blood.

"There's no fool like an old fool," she said silently, as the doctor motioned her into the room. Now, crossing to the bed, Casandra couldn't help thinking that the cancerous cells in her husband were cooperating so splendidly.

"Jason, love," she murmured, and bending over him to kiss his creased forehead. "I've missed you."

Through sunken and pain-racked eyes the rancher gazed up at his wife. His skin was ashy, the flesh gone from it and hanging loosely along his sunken jawline. The salt and pepper hair was completely white now, giving Jason McClintock a ghostly appearance. The hands folded over the covering sheet were wasted, mottled with liver spots, but there was enough strength remaining for him to pat her gently on the cheek.

"How was the ride?" he asked weakly.

"Ox and I had a wonderful time. Did you realize, love, that you have some prehistoric sites on your land."

He laughed weakly. "I'm a prehistoric site."

"Well, Doctor Travis, can my husband entertain his guests?"

"Of course I can. Travis, here, wants me to lay off the whiskey and cigars. Hogwash! Both of you know that's all that keeps me going."

"I defer to the good doctor."

"Very well, but only one cigar a day."

"You forgot the booze, doc!" he snorted defiantly.

"One shot glass a day."

"Won't even wet my whistle," protested McClintock. "Okay, you two, send up Parker. Oh, how was Andy's day?"

"Missed his daddy," gushed Casandra. "But building sand castles and crabbing about having to wear short pants. He insists upon wearing levis just like the hands." They laughed together. "Just like his daddy."

McClintock's eyes sparkled. "Damn right. That yonker will make a better rancher than his pa. Well, scat, you two."

The guests had deserted the main house for a garden patio which was lighted by Chinese lanterns. Servants drifted back and forth, bringing fresh drinks and trays of tidbits to the guests, and from a little alcove formed by weeping willows came the lilting strains of a Mexican band. The moon stood full over the Power River flood basin, brushing back some of the darkness. Into their midst swept Casandra, to go over to Tom Lamont, the segundo of the Mac spread, a tall, courteous man. "How's it going?"

"Mighty fine, Cassie. How's the boss?"

"He'll be here."

A smile swept across Lamont's long, bony face. "This party wouldn't be the same without him."

They parted, with the other women seeking out Casandra to offer their condolences as to her husband's health and to offer a helping hand if that became necessary. Somehow, she managed to endure the small talk, brightened some when Jason McClintock was pushed out onto the patio in a wheelchair by the major-domo. With the others, she went to his side, stood there while the thirty or so guests told the rancher how good it was to see him again.

"Jason," said a rancher, "where did you pick up this brandy?"

"Imported stuff from Ireland."

"Damn, it sure goes down smooth."

McClintock glowered in the presence of old acquaintances, and when dinner was announced, was rolled by the major-domo to the head of a long table, and with Casandra settling down by his right hand. She was on her fifth glass of whiskey, and was more relaxed now, and talking openly with those around her at the table. Tantalizing plates of barbecued beef were placed before the guests, the Mexican band kept playing, the night grew older.

Sometime later, Casandra swung onto the patio to dance with the segundo, and with others who asked, but the strain of coming down here to the party proved to be too much for Jason McClintock, and he bid a reluctant goodnight to everyone before leaving.

"Don't stop the party," he told them, "on my account. My missus won't let that happen. See you in the morning."

The rancher's departure slowed the party for a few minutes, then the tempo resumed. As Casandra danced, she caught a glimpse of Ox McClintock hovering in the shadows, knew that he wouldn't show himself. Some of the Mac hands wandered over. Around two o'clock, she slipped away to seek the quiet of her room.

Entering her bedroom, Casandra moved to a table and lighted a lamp. She frowned at the open terrace door, knowing that she'd ordered it closed, and with irritated strides she went there, only to pause when an alien aroma wafted into her nostrils.

"Tobacco smoke?" she questioned. The heady aroma was familiar to her, and then she blurted out, "Damn that Killane, he's back!" To a swirl of velvet she swept out onto the terrace to find Navajo Killane sprawled in a wicker chair, the glow from his cigarette revealing the sardonic glint in his green eyes. "You bastard, just where in hell have you been?"

"If I knew you missed me that much," Killane said after a while, "I'd have stayed away longer."

"Well?"

"Been around," he said vaguely.

"You knew I wanted you to take me to Cheyenne."

"Hadn't forgotten. Should be an interesting trip."

"You're up to something—"

"One thing I like about you, Mrs. McClintock, is that suspicious nature. Come here."

She curled onto his lap, threw an arm around his neck, ran her fingers through the shaggy black hair. Within a few moments she was aroused, wanting him, seeking his wide mouth with her parted lips.

"You never seem to get enough."

"Navajo," she hissed, "you've got a crude mouth." Her hand snaked under his shirt to stroke the hard chest muscles. His musky Indian smell filled her nostrils. She brought her mouth to his neck and bit him lightly, possessively.

"A black widow, that's what you are."

"You love it, Navajo." Rising, she reached for his

163

hand. "Come on, lover, it's getting late."

Killane rose, flipped the cigarette down, ground it out under the heel of his boot before going with her into the bedroom, where Casandra pulled the covers down on the bed and began undressing. Dropping his hat by the lighted lamp, he reached to turn it out, only to have her murmur, "Leave it on. I want to see what I'm going to enjoy tonight."

Shrugging out of his black leather vest, he replied, "Like I said, maybe I should stay away longer next time. But black widow or no, here I come."

As Casandra and her lover slipped into bed and one another's arms, they were unaware of a whisper of sound coming from the south wall, of a pair of eyes gazing at them through a concealed panel. In those eyes there was anguish, a deep and abiding pain that bespoke of betrayal.

In the adjoining bedroom, Jason McClintock closed the panel and let the picture fall back into place to cover it. He turned shakily to look at the major-demo, who held out a steadying arm. "Sir," Desmond Parker said gently, "I wish now I hadn't told you about Killane going to her room."

"No, no," the rancher said bitterly, and going back to drop onto his bed in a sitting position. "You did right by me, Desmond . . . you did right."

"If you want, I'll take care of him—"

"I know you would, my old friend. "But I want no killing done on the Mac spread. It's my fault . . . knew this had been going on for some time."

"Then you must do something about it," Parker insisted.

"No! She gave me a son. Anyway, Desmond, I still

have some time left. Time to ensure that my son gets the ranch. Men like Killane have a way of getting themselves killed. But I shall not have a hand in it."

"I don't understand? You've always been a fighter, Mr. McClintock."

"Because of my wife. Because I still treasure the pleasure she's given me. Or perhaps because I'm a dying old fool, Desmond. Now, to hell with my doctor, pour me another glass of whiskey; to the brim, Desmond, damnit, to the brim. And help yourself to some."

19

The wind coming in off the endless plains seemed to have the railhead city of Cheyenne as its particular target, laid out as it was in the open and with no sheltering buttes or mesas, that, and the swirling dust which accompanied Long Henry into town, stinging his eyes and powdering his clothes and face. With the coming of nightfall the wind let up, died away completely when the moon rose from the east to began its lonesome trek across the star-studded expanse of sky.

Long Henry secured lodging at the Cimmaron House, an elegant hotel of brick construction nestled among shops and banks and saloons. The first order of business for both him and Deacon O'Shay had been a hot bath. Next came a new suit for O'Shay, but Long Henry put on his worn traveling clothes — western trousers, flannel shirt and vest, weathered Stetson.

"I'm craving some action," said O'Shay.

"Go ahead. Find a game."

"You look worried, partner."

"Mostly about you, Deacon."

"Me? This old renegade sure as hell don't need no

chaperon."

"I've got a hunch this is Navajo Killane's stomping grounds. Remember, one of those men who tried to bushwhack us got away. Figure he came here to warn Killane."

"Been thinking about that. Kind of strange you being told in Deadwood that the gunslinger would be here."

"Sure is hard to figure out."

"I'll let you ponder the imponderable, Henry. Don't wait up."

Shortly after O'Shay had left their suite, Long Henry buckled on his holstered revolver. He checked his appearance in the dresser mirror, saw the worry on his face, more of it for O'Shay than himself. For certain he looked older. Impulsively, he unbuttoned a shirt button, pulled out the locket and studied his wife's picture. Something told him that she was still alive, that all of the pieces would come together here in Cheyenne. A pensive smile tugged at his mouth as he recalled her saying often how she hated cold weather. Winters in these parts were hellish on man and beast, he knew, but outside it was hot, and by his reckoning would get hotter before too many days passed.

Outside the Cimmaron House, he set off down the street without any apparent destination in mind. As he walked, Long Henry studied the brands on those horses hitched to tie rails. He could have gone to the sheriff and inquired there, but an inner caution told him not to be too inquisitive, that sooner or later he'd spot a horse carrying the Rocking MC brand.

His search through the many streets proved to be fruitless, and the next day Long Henry went over to the railroad tracks and followed them to where cattle were being herded out of holding pens and loaded onto railroad cars, their ultimate destination the packing houses in Chicago. He wandered around the pens while checking the brands on the cattle, and on the few horses being used.

That evening, out in front of the Cimmaron House, he listened to Deacon O'Shay complaining about having been talked into going to the opera house. "Partner," said O'Shay, "went to one of them places down in Albuquerque — ears rang for a week afterwards. This ain't one of your better ideas."

"You need a little culture. Besides, I'm getting tired of looking for that Rocking MC brand and waiting for Killane to show."

Walking downstreet, they glanced into lighted shops or at the faces of others out for an evening stroll. Crossing to the opposite side, their boots sounded hollowly on the planking running in front of the Grand Hotel. In the next block was the opera house where carriages were disgorging passengers.

"See them fancy rigs," complained O'Shay. "Turns my knees to jelly. I need some fortification before I join that crowd." He swung toward inviting batwings, entered the Delmonico Saloon, and Long Henry had no choice but that of going after O'Shay and joining him at the bar, where O'Shay ordered for them.

"You say," came a deep booming voice from some tables along the back wall, "that you went and tossed a bull!"

Through the mirror behind the bar Long Henry could see the reflection of the man who'd spoken, judging from the buckskins, beaver hat and flowing beard that he was a trapper, or possibly a mountain man.

"Threw that bull to the dirt in nine seconds," bragged the other man at the table. He shoved his workworn Stetson to the back of his head, and slopped beer on his leather vest when he lifted the stein to drink from it. His dark leather chaps were adorned at the outer fringes with large Mexican coins.

"Your mammy," retorted the man wearing buckskins, "probably gave you a little tom cat when you was in short pants, but Charley Blackman here has got a grizzly bear for a pet."

"Shit, Blackman, you're all brag . . . and that nine feet wide."

"Up in the mountains," roared Blackman, "we've got eight hour echoes."

"Now just what in blue blazes is an eight hour echo?"

"Before rolling up in my buffalo robe at night, this here child sets his alarm clock by shouting, 'Time to get up'."

Laughter erupted from those at the other tables, the men lining the bar, and the cowhand, his face reddening and showing anger, sprang up from his chair and headed toward the back door, muttering, "Damn liar!"

"Liar am I!" The mountain man rose ponderously. "No simple-minded Mac hand is going to call Charley Blackman a liar." He hurried after the cowhand.

"Mac hand?" Long Henry said to himself, and he turned to the man standing to his right. "What did he mean . . . Mac hand?"

The man shrugged, muttered, "Just an expression."

Fastening a large hand on the man's shirt front,

Long Henry pulled him close, said grimly, "Tell me what it means?"

"That hand" the man stammered, "rides for the Mac spread."

"Whereabouts is it?"

"Up by the Bighorns—Jason McClintock's place."

He could feel his temples pounding as he turned back to his drink and placed his hands on the bar top while trying to go down the backtrail of time and sort the name of Jason McClintock from all the others, both on the wandering trail and in Waco. He'd heard that name before, that was for sure, and though he still couldn't put a face to that name, the Frontier Hotel in Waco came to mind. Of course, the man Casandra had pointed out to him in the dining room, and now he recalled her dancing with the rancher afterwards. So after all these years the truth had surfaced. The rancher must have killed the merchant, Jed Bullock, set fire to his house, then forced Casandra to go with him. It was the only rational explanation he could think of, but somehow it didn't set right in his mind. Who had paid Killane to bushwhack him? He had to clear his head, get out of here, and Long Henry wheeled away from the bar and lunged toward the batwings.

Deacon O'Shay put down his glass without drinking its contents. He'd overheard Long Henry talking to the stranger at the bar, knew that Long Henry would go looking for that Mac hand. But when he was outside, it was to find that his partner had disappeared. The worry that Henry Banner would head up to McClintock's ranch revealed itself in O'Shay's eyes. It was showdown time; he pondered over how the years had hammered his partner down, aged him, the loss of his wife tearing the man's heart out. From what he'd seen of Casandra down in Waco, and being a shrewd judge of character besides, O'Shay couldn't help thinking that she'd had a hand in all of this.

"She must have been sired by the devil . . . to do a man like this."

The gambler knew there would be killing now, but he'd sided with his partner in tight spots before, and besides, this was not the time to cut and run.

"Yup, for certain the hunt for her had to end some time."

20

The cavalcade of riders, eleven strong, and not including the two pack horses, had left the Mac spread two days ago, camping the first night at a wide and windy spot called Reno Junction, and again last night just northeast of the Laramies. Casandra McClintock rode western-style, and was glad to be away from the ranch. It was highly unlikely that a roving band of Indians or outlaws on the prowl would attack their party, but each man rode with his eyes scanning the distant landscape.

"Tell me, Navajo, how come you always smoke the same brand of tobacco?"

"Brings back old memories."

"Of New Orleans," she said distastefully.

He grinned at her around his cigarette. "You never seemed to mind before."

Casandra could see the challenge in his eyes. He was arrogant, headstrong, totally unpredictable. And expendable, she was realizing. Her plans were to spend at least a week in Cheyenne, and after that go by stagecoach down to Denver. There, so she'd been told, a hired gun could be found. But did she really want

Killane out of the way? He proved useful in the past, was willing to take risks for her. Casandra knew that she'd changed, as had the times. Lawyers with black leather briefcases and tight little smiles were becoming the new gunslingers of the west, wracking more havoc in a courtroom than could a band of rustlers. In Cheyenne, she'd acquire the services of a lawyer, one who wasn't known to her husband. And the geologist would be there.

When they loped over a rise, a column of dust could be seen to their front, and one of the hands shouted that it was a stagecoach heading into Cheyenne, and Casandra asked, "How much further is it?"

"Another five miles and we'll be there."

Around mid-afternoon they followed the stagecoach into Cheyenne, where they walked their horses through the streets and drew up by the Grand Hotel. Casandra's luggage was removed from the pack horses, carried inside by Killane and another hand. She signed the register, then went with the others and the desk clerk up to the second floor, where the clerk ushered them into her suite. The clerk and the other hand left to go downstairs, and Casandra moved over to the corner bar and helped herself to some brandy. "I have to see some people."

Killane crunched out his cigarette in an ashtray, said matter-of-factly, "Your business."

"I won't be able to see you tonight."

"Them's the breaks, I reckon." Hitching at his gun belt, he passed through the door and went into the hallway.

Navajo Killane left his horse at the livery stable where the other Mac hands had stabled their mounts.

He went alone to a saloon located in the Chinese section to keep a rendezvous with the two hands he'd left behind in Deadwood. When his eyes grew accustomed to the dim light, he saw Cal Petrie motioning to him from a booth, and Killane went there. Petrie, he noticed right away, had been drinking heavily.

"Wondered when you'd get here," Petrie mumbled.

Killane settled down facing the front bar, behind which a Chinese barkeep was wiping some glasses. At a secluded table two more Chinese sat stoically, the sweet aroma of the opium they were smoking coming back to Killane. He said, "Where's Talbot?"

"Got hisself killed."

"I'm listening?"

"Up the trail a piece. Told him not to do it."

"Do what?"

"Try to hold up them gamblers. Talbot got gunned down, he did. Lucky I got away."

Inwardly, Killane was livid with rage, and Petrie failed to notice the chilling glint in Killane's narrowed eyes when he picked up the bottle and drank some more whiskey. The breed knew that Petrie was of no further use to him, and alive, could tie him in with the attempted robbery of the gold train, not to mention the other jobs they'd pulled in the Black Hills.

"You manage to find out where the gamblers are staying?"

"Cimmaron House." Petrie's grin revealed the gaps between his yellowed teeth as he pushed the bottle toward Killane. "Have a snort."

"Sure," he muttered, as he half-rose. "Nothing like drinking with an old pal." Quickly, he clamped a hand over Petrie's mouth, with the other hand holding a knife and coming in low. Petrie stiffened in shock when the blade slid deep into his stomach, and Killane held it there until the man went limp. Then gently he lowered Petrie's head onto the table as he pulled out his knife, to wipe the blood on the blade on Petrie's shirt, and calmly Navajo Killane sauntered out the way he had come.

Casandra McClintock stepped down from the carriage and went with her lawyer into the Alexandra, one of Cheyenne's better restaurants. Their wait in the anteroom was only momentary, and during which time she asked about the geologist, Aaron Van Cleve.

"Comes from wealth," said Marcus Zenin. He was middle-aged and wearing a dark vested suit and four-in-hand tie along with the ritualistic cowboy boots.

"How interesting."

Then a waiter escorted them into the crowded dining room. Lighted chandeliers hung from a high ceiling of ornate pressed tin painted a mellow white color. On the round table were lacy white tablecloths and fancy silverware, while the chairs grouped around each table were blue padded and had arms, and blue velvet drapes covered the many windows.

"Mrs. McClintock, it's my pleasure to introduce Mr. Van Cleve."

The geologist rose gracefully and smiled into Casandra's eyes before reaching for her hand and bestowing on it a kiss, and she was reluctant to have him let go. He's simply divine, she thought. He had blond handsome looks and there were flecks of gold in his blue eyes. The expensive summer suit clung to his lithe

175

frame. "My pleasure, Mrs. McClintock. Mr. Zenin has told me so much about you."

Before she realized it, Van Cleve had pulled out a chair for her, and with a grateful smile she sat down. It was with some difficulty that she pulled her eyes from the geologist and turned to the lawyer. She'd found out that Marcus Zenin had a reputation for a certain shrewdness, could be ruthless if the situation called for it, so she'd hired him. But his appearance was deceiving. The face was long and fleshy, had a look of gentle benevolence about it, around the eyes were crinkles, the lower lip was big and pendulous, almost woman-like in its shape, this, and he had a mane of silvery hair. She could almost visualize the lawyer mounting a pulpit, hear church bells chiming.

As if reading her thoughts, Zenin said, "I explained to Mr. Van Cleve just what was required of him. And, Mr. Van Cleve, you stated that you would render your decision at this time?"

"I must admit that I had some reservations about leaving Philadelphia." His eyes went to Casandra "Misplaced feelings, I might add. Back east, Mrs. McClintock, you'd be the belle of the ball."

Flushing with pleasure, Casandra murmured, "Why, thank you." Already she knew that this attractive young man would work for her. He was poised, charming, and she knew that he was single. The dossier he'd sent spoke of wealth and breeding. Though Aaron Van Cleve wasn't aware of it now, there would come a day when he would play a larger role in her plans. Was he any good in bed? Casandra found herself blushing at the thought, and smiled when the wine steward came out of an alcove and toward their table.

"I took the liberty of ordering some wine," Van Cleve told them.

"Chalenay," beamed the lawyer Zenin.

As the meal progressed, the geologist opened up to questions asked by Casandra, and she listened raptly to what life was like back east. And she was aware of his growing interest in her, especially when she told of her husband's illness.

"Well, you two seem to be getting along splendidly," said Marcus Zenin. "If you'll excuse me, I'll run along. But I'll leave my carriage at your disposal, Mrs. McClintock."

"Mr. Zenin," she said, "you've been most cooperative. I'll drop by tomorrow to discuss this new oil venture in greater detail."

When Casandra and the geologist left the restaurant, it was to go for a carriage ride. Outside Cheyenne, and where the stagecoach road slithered down a rocky height on its way south to Denver, Casandra ordered the driver to pull over. Van Cleve clambered down, helped her to the ground, and together they strolled past the jumble of cactus and to the edge of a precipice. The Milky Way's wide band of stars stood above them.

"Just what do you know about the oil business?"

"Just that you have to do a lot of drilling to get at it," said Van Cleve.

"Oil is my future, Aaron. May I call you that?"

"Please, do."

"When you get to the ranch, I'll introduce you as a professor of . . . of biology. Seems my husband wants nothing to do with the oil business. Anyway, you'll

177

have the run of the ranch. Just tell my lawyer what you need in the way of equipment, manpower."

"It will be expensive, I'm afraid."

"Money is no object. One must take certain risks."

"Yes, one must."

Casandra could feel her breath quickening, the look on his smooth-shaven face telling her that this could be a tempestuous relationship. The first move was up to her, she knew, and her response to what showed on his face was to murmur boldly, "I want you to kiss me."

Wordlessly, he removed his low-crowned hat and gathered her in his arms.

There was no lost love between Navajo Killane and the hands Casandra had brought along with her to Cheyenne. He was more or less the ramrod on this trip, relaying to the others what she wanted done. But for two days now she'd spent most of her time with that greenhorn of a geologist, while the other Mac hands were scattered to hell and gone around town. And he'd spotted the former marshal of Waco yesterday, and in the company of the gambler, O'Shay. The trick was to get Banner and his wife together, or at least have Casandra get a glimpse of her first husband. In his mind, Killane was going over what to do, and relishing, too, that unexpected confrontation.

"She'll damn well believe in ghosts when that happens," he muttered, studying the poker hand he'd just been dealt.

He couldn't recall the name of the saloon he was in at the moment, nor how much he'd had to drink, and to add teeth to his resentment was this losing streak.

"Gimme three cards." Picking up his shot glass, he banged it on the card table. "A refill!"

In the game with Killane were two railroad men, a cowhand, and a drummer who had the nasty habit of clicking his false teeth every time he was dealt some good cards. That's about all Killane had heard this afternoon, those clicking teeth, the rasping sound of cards being shuffled and low comments among the players, and a sleeping drunk passing wind from where he was stretched out on the barroom's only pool table.

"Click-Click—Click-Click-Click—"

One of the railroad workers glared at the drummer, as did Killane, but he was too concerned with what Casandra was doing at the moment than this penny ante poker game, and he threw his cards down and left the table. He found a bar where men's teeth didn't click and the air was somewhat better, and over a bottle of rotgut Navajo Killane began working himself up to getting half-shot, as the Sioux Indians called it.

21

Sooner or later, pondered Long Henry, the gunslinger would show up in Cheyenne. From a local he'd found out the best route to Jason McClintock's MC ranch. Confronting Casandra could wait until his business here was over.

It was coming onto mid-morning, and getting sultry, with a few clouds starting to build up into something bigger. He'd been out by this meandering creek since sunup, cutting loose with his revolver at some empty cans he'd brought along. His draw was getting quick and smooth, but according to that local, Navajo Killane was greased lightning. What happened, happened, he figured. But Long Henry was harder than he'd been in Waco, and with nothing to distract his mind or eye, only the need to have it out with Killane.

Along with the tin cans, he'd brought with him some fishing gear, a rod and reel and creel, and during the time he'd been practicing his draw, the ripples on the water told him this was a likely spot to try his hand at fishing. This used to be one of his favorite pastimes. But when he tried casting, he discovered the old skills weren't there, and it took several casts before he managed to bring the plug near a little overhang, and he settled down on the thick grass and waited for something to happen.

As he reached for the makings, the water rippled, the line snapped tight, and in his excitement he dropped his pouch and tobacco paper. He set the hook, started reeling in the line, and to his delight found that he'd caught a trout. He kept on fishing until the position of the sun told him it was around noon, then with some reluctance he mounted up and headed back to Cheyenne.

The ride back was uneventful. Stabling his horse, he took the fishing gear with him on the short walk back to the Cimmaron Hotel, where he went into the kitchen and returned the fishing gear, but taking the creel with him up to his suite. As expected, Deacon O'Shay, was still in bed, having played poker most of the night.

"Well, pardner, it's time to rise and shine," said Long Henry through an impish grin, and saying that, he opened the creel and dumped the fish he'd caught onto the sleeping O'Shay.

The gambler came awake sputtering and recoiling from the sight of several pairs of unblinking eyes gaping at him and trying to squirm away from the slimy feel of the fish. "Damn," he snorted testily, "for a moment there I had the notion my first and only wife had caught up with me. You tetched in the head, doing that?" Gingerly, he brushed a trout off his chest and swung his legs to the floor.

"Trouble with you, Deacon, is that you don't appreciate the finer things of life."

"Sleeping with trout don't qualify among the finer things of life, Mr. Banner."

"Well, just supposing I take these fish down to the kitchen. Now you wouldn't object to a fine meal of trout, would you, and I'll buy the wine, too."

"You drive a hard bargain." O'Shay scratched at an itch on his neck.

"But tend to it."

"You're sure hard to please."

O'Shay laughed as he rose and pounded Long Henry on the back. "Seeing as how I like trout, a deal."

Casandra responded to the soft knock on the door with a puzzled frown. She wasn't expecting Van Cleve until later tonight, nor anyone else for that matter. Pulling a robe over her chemise, she left the bedroom and swept over the circular rug to the door, and opened it to meet the concerned look of a Mac hand; Spencer, she thought. "Yes?"

With economical grace the cowhand removed his hat and said shyly, "Don't mean to bother you, ma'am, but there's something I think you should know."

She motioned him into her suite, closed the door.

"Talked to a carpetbagger just arrived from Deadwood. This gent says that some of your men were mixed up in a robbery up thataway. Leastwise, that's the talk. No way of proving otherwise, 'cause those who were got themselves killed."

"I see." Casandra had the feeling that some of the

men who rode around with Killane had a hand in this, and she added, "Did they identify the men?"

"Carpetbagger didn't mention no names. But there's been a tall gent going around asking about Killane, too."

"Navajo couldn't be mixed up in that," she said defensively.

"Just figured you should know, is all."

"Thank you . . . Spencer." She let him out of the suite, went to the corner bar and fixed herself a drink, and settled thoughtfully on an overstuffed chair. Perhaps she wouldn't have to hire someone to take care of Killane. He had to be mixed up with that robbery. She could send a telegram to the authorities over there, telling them where to find Killane. On the other hand, let nature take its course. Navajo drank too much, and she'd heard that he cheated at cards. It would probably only be a matter of time before someone he cheated gunned him down or he came down with liver problems, but even through her present disenchantment with Killane she had to admit he'd been a great lover.

A tall man asking about Killane?

Suddenly, as if a veil had been lifted from her mind, came the name of Henry Banner. And she felt a chill come over her. Hurriedly she emptied the glass, made another drink. Dammit, why couldn't the past stay buried! This was all Killane's fault, her only link with all that had happened before. He was destroying her, but he wouldn't get away with it. Oh, why couldn't she get it straight in her mind about him. If only Stephen Van Cleve was here, as he'd been until the early hours

183

of the morning, comforting her. Grimacing, she set her glass aside, realizing that this was no time for liquor, and returned to the bedroom to prepare herself for the night.

22

Navajo Killane swaggered into the Grand Hotel. He'd sobered up some, and despite the pounding headache, the cotton sticking to the roof of his mouth, he was feeling good about himself. The night clerk came around the counter to intercept the gunslinger, pulled up with a frightened abruptness when Killane made as if to draw his holstered gun. The clerk paled, wanting the sanctuary behind his counter, but was too afraid to move.

Killane laughed jeeringly. "Just sashay back to your hole, gopher." His spur-jangling boots found the staircase. She wasn't expecting him, and anyway, this would be his last go-around with Casandra McClintock. He knew the black widow had gotten to that tenderfoot of a geologist, but somehow it didn't matter anymore. He'd come here to pass the collection plate.

A couple came out of a second-floor room and gave Killane a wide berth as he sauntered past them. He reeked of booze and other assorted odors from not having taken a bath for a considerable length of time, and the woman wrinkled her nose before scurrying down the steps with her husband. Easing up to the door leading into Casandra's suite, Killane turned the door knob to find that the door wasn't locked. He cat-footed inside, smiled when he heard her moving about in her bedroom. He lowered himself onto the corner of a table on which papers were scattered, reached for the pouch of Perique. Now he could hear Casandra humming a song that she used to sing to him. Dragging smoke into his lungs, he waited patiently.

In her bedroom, Casandra put a dab of perfume behind each ear, adjusted one of the red pendant earrings while glancing at the clock. Van Cleve would be here in less than an hour, then they'd have supper with her lawyer. The plans for the oil drilling operation were almost completed, and this thought pleased her, as did the young geologist.

"Mrs. Stephen Van Cleve." The name sounded right on her lips, and proper. Why, they could spend summers on the Continent, winter down south. And she knew of a man in Denver who specialized in genealogies. Having a marquis or a baron for an ancestor would make her more presentable to Stephen's parents. After all, it wouldn't do to tell them that she was the daughter of a West Virginia wildcatter. Frowning, she glanced about as she became aware of an alien aroma, but yet, a familiar one.

"Killane's here!" she muttered in disgust.

Springing to her feet, Casandra moved around the bed and into the other room, became angrier when she saw the sardonic smile on his face, and somewhat uneasy too, for in his green eyes was a strange glitter, as if Navajo Killane was privy to some dark secret.

"I haven't time for you now," she said irritably.

"Got all the time in the world, Cassie gal."

"All right, Navajo, speak your piece." Crossing to the bar, and not wanting to show him how disturbed she was by his unexpected appearance here, she poured herself a steadying drink.

He let a smoke ring issue from between his lips, feeling a pure joy at what he was about to tell her. "You're mighty uppity for a woman who's got two husbands."

Casandra dropped the ice cube, blurted out, "What the hell are you talking about?"

"They jail bigamists in this territory."

"Get out of here!" she yelled. Picking up her glass, she threw it at him, and he moved to evade it, the smile widening to show all of his gold-gleaming teeth.

"Come over to this window, black widow."

"I told you to . . ."

Killane shouted back: "You ain't telling me nothing no more! I sent a note to a gent who's staying at the Cimmaron House. Along about now he'll be waiting down in front of that millinery shop across the street." Killane crossed to her, grabbed her arm, forcibly made her walk with him to a window overlooking the street in front of the Grand Hotel. Though the millinery shop was closed for the night, out front there was a street lamp.

"This gent's an old friend of yours, black widow. Should be along any minute now."

Casandra tried to free her arm, only to have Killane slap her viciously across the face. She cried out in pain, swore at him. "You damned animal," she hissed.

"Take a look, black widow!"

Almost of their own volition her eyes centered on a tall man moving along the street, and when he reached the millinery shop, he stopped in shadows, stood there for several suspenseful minutes before coming forward to stand in the glow of the street lamp, and Casandra's knees buckled when she realized that it was her first husband, Henry Banner.

"No!" she screamed out, and tearing her arm out of Killane's grasp. "He's dead! You killed him!" The color had left her face, and her eyes were wide with the knowledge of what this meant.

"Thought I did," he said coldly.

"You bastard," she raged, "you lied to me!"

"You're right about one thing," said Killane, and backhanded her across the face, "this breed is a bastard for sure." He grabbed a hunk of her hair, and smiling tightly, brought her over to the table where the papers were, forced her to sit in a chair. "Now, Cassie gal, I want you to make me a bank draft for say . . . twenty thousand dollars."

"Damn you, no!"

Cupping a hand under her chin, he twisted her head sideways and up so that they were eyeing one another—the gunslinger, the former prostitute—and she realized that she was trapped in a web of her own making, with the lust to kill showing clear in Killane's eyes. "Twenty thousand for starters," he said. He ruffled through the papers, found the form he wanted and placed it before her on the table, and from the inkwell he took out a quilled pen, handed it to her.

Casandra could still feel the sting of those slaps; blood trickled from one corner of her mouth. With a shaking hand, and tears forming now, she filled out the bank draft. At the far end of the table was her handbag, and in it a derringer. Somehow, she had to end this right now, tend to Henry Banner later.

Killane picked up the bank draft. "Always knew you'd help me strike it big." He pulled a folded piece of paper out of a shirt pocket, tossed it before her. "Opened a bank account here. Every month, woman, you'll deposit a thousand dollars in it. You miss a payment, a letter gets sent to your rancher husband. Yeah, and so will that geologist fella, Van Cleve, hear about little Mrs. Bigamist. Best thing that damn fool can do is to skedaddle back east. Been fun bedding you, black widow, but I'm getting while the getting's good." A mocking laugh came from the gunslinger as he swung around and headed toward the door.

Easing out of the chair, Casandra slipped around the table to her purse, out of which she pulled the derringer. She grasped it with both hands, brought it to bear on Killane's back. "Bastard!" she said, as she pulled the trigger.

Killane staggered from the impact of the slug piercing his upper back. The second slug hit near his spinal cord, emptying her weapon, and she stumbled backwards as Killane struggled to turn around even as his right hand was pulling out his revolver. Now he was facing her, the shock of what had happened planted on his hate-twisted face.

"Damn you . . . black widow." Slowly the gun came to bear on her, but before he could pull the trigger, the light went out of his eyes and he toppled forward and lay still.

Casandra stepped forward and sagged against the table. She was breathing heavily while sweat glistened on her forehead. It was over, she realized, done and over. Had anyone heard the shots? The bank draft!

She shoved the derringer into her purse and scurried around the table. Crouching down by his inert form, she pulled the bank draft out of his shirt pocket along with the pouch of Perique.

"You should have stayed in New Orleans," she said triumphantly, and with a bitter smile she threw the pouch into a corner, came erect, let her thoughts settle down while trying to determine her next course of action. First, check to see if Henry Banner was still there, and she hurried back to the window to find that he was still lingering in front of the millinery shop. Now Casandra went to the door and peered out into the hallway; it was empty.

Locking the door, she hurried into her bedroom, the clock telling her that Van Cleve would be here in about ten minutes. There was no time for him now. Hurriedly she changed into riding clothes. The murder would have to be pinned on Henry Banner, and she would need the help of her men. Where did the Mac hands hang out? Yes, that Irish bar; George's Office. As for her wardrobe, she would have to leave it behind.

Hurrying back into the adjoining room, she scooped up the papers littering the table, carried them into the bathroom. Most of them detailed the oil drilling operation, and if she left them behind it was entirely possible that they could wind up in Jason McClintock's hands. She dropped them in the bathtub, lit a match, which she dropped onto the papers.

In the chilling excitement of what had just happened, she'd forgotten about Killane's hitting her, and glancing in the wall mirror, saw that her makeup was smeared, while the blood on her lips tasted salty in her mouth. Quickly she washed her face and combed her hair. She would have one of her men look up the geologist, tell him to come up to the ranch, where she could explain this.

Casandra slipped into the hallway. She left the door ajar, wanting the body to be found while Henry Banner was still in the vicinity. Hesitating, she wondered if perhaps it would be better to stay here, tell the marshal of Cheyenne that Henry Banner had come up here, found her with Killane, and out of jealousy shot the man. But how could she explain the years of separation? She found the back staircase, and out behind the hotel hurried southward down an alley. Only when Casandra was several blocks away from the Grand Hotel and nearing the saloon where the Mac hands were known to hang out did she begin to control the fear which still pounded at her temples.

"I hope they hang Banner for this," she said stonily. Wait a minute, she mused, there is another way, and then she was entering the saloon.

23

Long Henry felt exposed where he waited under the glowing street lamp. The note said that Casandra would meet him here. Or maybe Killane had sent it, was even now sighting down the barrel of a rifle. But it was a chance Long Henry had to take. What could he possibly say to his wife? His love for her had eroded. Though there was still an ache in his heart, the years without her had changed him. He began comparing her to that woman he'd met in Deadwood, Molly Corcoran. A difficult task, he realized, because he knew now that he'd never really known Casandra, that she had sought him out.

Impatience gnawing at him, Long Henry stared again at the Grand Hotel opposite. Could it be possible that the note had drawn him here so that Casandra would be able to observe him from the hotel? Figuring that it was worth checking out, he crossed over and entered the lobby.

"Could you tell me if a Mrs. McClintock is staying here?"

"Certainly," the night clerk said. "She has the Governor's Suite."

"Is she in?"

"I believe so, sir."

"Obliged." Long Henry went to the staircase and moved up it to the second floor. Glancing to his left, he noticed light seeping through an open door, and he headed that way. The gilded plate on the door told him this was her suite, and he knocked tentatively. He waited only momentarily before easing the door open. He stared hard at the body, then stepped around it and looked in the other rooms. She was gone, and he went back and rolled the dead man onto his back.

"Killane?" he muttered in disbelief. "Guess someone beat me to him."

He stood up. For certain he didn't want someone to find him in here. Maybe Killane had sent that note after all, letting him wait out front so that Casandra could see him. Maybe this was a case of thieves falling out. When he'd asked the clerk if Mrs. McClintock was staying here, he should have shown the man the picture he had of Casandra. It could be that she wasn't married to the rancher, but that chance was damned slim, now that he'd found Killane's body up here.

Moving to the door, he paused to glance back, and murmured, "If she killed him, I wondered if she pulled out his gold teeth."

Long Henry started down the hallway and slowed his pace when a blond-haired man came off the staircase. He stared at the bouquet of red roses the man was holding, the hunch coming to him that this blue-eyed stranger was here to see Casandra.

"Maybe you could help me?"

"Sir?" said Van Cleve.

He pulled out the locket and opened it to show Van

Cleve the picture of his wife. "Is this Mrs. McClintock?"

"Yes it is. Why?"

"A word of advice," Long Henry said harshly. "You'll be damned lucky if all she costs you is a dozen red roses. If I was you, stranger, I'd hightail it out of here, pronto!" One long stride carried Long Henry to the staircase.

Stephen Van Cleve stood there for a moment, a bewildered look on his face, and with a wondering shake of his head he continued on down the hallway toward Casandra's suite. The door was wide open, and with an anticipatory smile he doffed his hat and glanced in, then recoiled in horror. He'd never seen a dead man before, at least not in a hotel suite, and a certain silence coming from the suite told him that no living person was in there. Still swimming in his mind were the warning words of the tall stranger. Backing away, the young geologist dropped the bouquet as though it had suddenly gotten hot and ran toward the staircase.

A pair of riders passed on the quiet street, and Long Henry glanced at them as he came off the boardwalk and headed for a saloon at the corner. By now, he reckoned, that young man he'd encountered in the hotel had gone to find the marshal. Somehow, he drew no solace from the death of Navajo Killane. Too long had he been savoring a showdown with the man. He fashioned a bitter grin, knowing that Casandra would have to do some tall talking to get herself out of this murder.

What manner of man was Jason McClintock? Down in Waco, the picture he'd presented to Long Henry had been one of dependability, trustworthiness. For the longest time he'd believed that the rancher had talked his wife into leaving Waco, but the recent events here and in Deadwood dispelled that notion.

"Love's blinding glare," he said. Casandra and the gunslinger must have been partners, and maybe more than that. For certain she could twist a man around her little finger, mess his mind up. She must have pulled the wool over Jason McClintock's eyes, because in reflecting back on it now, Long Henry knew the man wasn't like-minded.

Back in Waco too, it was entirely possible that Casandra had killed that merchant, burned the house down herself, and up here the pattern was repeated, the dead man in her suite, the ashes he'd found in the bathtub. She wouldn't stay here, especially now that she knew he was alive, probably make tracks for the only sanctuary she had left, the Mac spread, as he would after he'd said his goodbyes to Deacon O'Shay.

The saloon was a big, rambling place where many of Cheyenne's money men hung out, and where big poker games were the rule rather than the exception. O'Shay wasn't seated at any of the tables, so Long Henry went over to the bar. "I'm looking for a friend, gambler named O'Shay?"

"Left," the barkeep said.

"How long ago?"

"Ten, fifteen minutes."

Outside, Long Henry moved upstreet. Generally, O'Shay played well into the night, and his leaving early could mean he wasn't feeling well. Could be, too, that his partner was seeing a woman. Turning the corner onto Cheyenne's main street, another thought struck Long Henry. If Casandra knew he was in town, she could try to have him killed. She knew where he was staying; the note he had received testified to that. And if O'Shay had gone to their suite, his life could be in danger.

He broke into a quicker walk, hoping that he was wrong about this, but Casandra's track record pretty much spoke for itself. It was highly unlikely that she and Killane had traveled alone all the way down here from the Big Horns. Between here and those mountains lay a stretch of rugged country, so those who'd acted as her escort were in town too. But they were mostly cowhands, not the kind of men who relished a shootout. She could lie to them, tell them he had killed Killane, and this thought carried him into the Cimmaron House, where the night clerk told him that Deacon O'Shay was upstairs, and Long Henry went to the staircase, attacked the steps two at a time.

Pow-Pow-Pow-Pow!

The rapid sound of gunfire came from the direction of Long Henry's suite, and he leaped forward onto the polished boards of the hallway and drew his weapon as he plunged toward his suite. Swinging the door open, he found O'Shay sagging to the floor, shards of broken window glass near him, and movement behind windows opening onto the balcony running around the second floor. A couple of bullets thudded into the wall near Long Henry, and he swept the lamp to the floor. He flopped down, firing at muzzle flashes coming from outside. A man yelled that he'd been hit.

Another hollered: "Let's vamoose!"

When Long Henry heard the sound of retreating boots, he shoved up from the floor and went to O'Shay. Hunkering down, he put an arm around his partner's shoulders, brought the man to a sitting position. Behind them, flames from the lamp were licking at the hardwood floor, and in the flickering light Long Henry grimaced at the blood staining the front of O'Shay's shirt.

The gambler coughed, struggled to open his eyes. "Well . . . pardner . . . seems we come across . . . hard times . . ."

"Don't talk, Deacon. I'll get a doctor."

Smiling wanly, O'Shay said weakly, "All I got is yours . . . pardner . . ." His eyes closed and he went limp in Long Henry's arms.

Bitterly, Long Henry lowered his partner to the floor, found a pitcher of water and threw its contents at the spreading fire, doused most of the flames, managed to stomp out the rest of them. Then he drew his revolver and slipped to a window to see that the wounded man on the balcony was struggling to rise. Opening the window, Long Henry crouched outside. He grabbed the man's shirt, said icily, "Who sent you?"

"Don't . . . don't shoot," the man gasped.

"You've got three seconds!"

"My boss . . . Mrs. McClintock . . ."

"Where is she?"

"Headed back to the ranch."

A cursory check by Long Henry revealed the wound to the man's side, and he said harshly, "You won't cash in your chips, mister. But you'll hang for this." He helped the man rise, then people were rushing into his suite, and a large man leaned out the window while

197

pointing his gun at the two men on the balcony.

"Far enough!" he said.

The wind came in gusts, shrilling through the oak trees scattered about the cemetery and sending dust-devils scurrying around the headstones. The undertaker whipped his team into motion, a squeaking noise coming from the wheels of his black wagon as he passed out of the cemetery and went down the road running the short distance to Cheyenne.

That left three people gazing solemnly at the pinewood coffin, the marshal of Cheyenne, the gravedigger, and a saddened Long Henry.

The marshal said: "Sorry to hear you won't accept the reward money that was posted on Navajo Killane."

Without looking at the man, Long Henry murmured, "Maybe you can give it to some orphanage."

"I'll do that." Realizing that he was still holding his hat, the marshal settled it over his head. "Still can't believe Mrs. McClintock killed the gunslinger."

"Believe it." Bending, Long Henry picked up some fresh dirt and threw it on Deacon O'Shay's coffin.

"Without any witnesses or weapon it'll be hard to prove, Mr. Banner. So you were married to her once?"

Long Henry put on his hat, turned to the marshal. "Still am, according to the law."

"Yes, she thought you were dead. I could go up there and bring her back here. But like I said, Mr. Banner, with no evidence my hands are tied."

"Reckon so," said Long Henry, and falling into step with the marshal as they moved toward their horses. Climbing into the saddle, he stared down at the man.

"On her orders I was gunned down by Killane. Can't prove it either . . . no more than you can prove the sun'll come up tomorrow morning."

"Then you're going after her?"

Nodding, Long Henry said, "Adios, marshal."

24

The heads of game animals covered one wall in Jason McClintock's study. The large room was full of subdued colors, mostly dark or light browns, and the curtains were drawn. McClintock sat behind his desk in his wheelchair. Lingering behind him was the major-domo, Desmond Parker. Their attention, that of the segundo, Tom Lamont, was on a man seated in a chair before the desk.

Mike Spencer was sweating, turning his hat nervously in his workworn hands, as he went on telling of what had happened in Cheyenne. "We was just following Mrs. McClintock's orders. She said this stranger, Henry Banner, broke into her suite, gunned down Killane. Said she managed to get away. Well, when someone you work with gets shot in the back . . . you got no choice . . ."

The segundo tapped Spencer on the shoulder, motioned for him to leave, and he did, hastening to the door and letting himself out, while the servant who'd been just outside listening ducked behind a china cabinet, and the cowpoke didn't see her as he found an outer door.

Inside the study, Jason McClintock lowered his head, placed his elbows on the arms of the wheelchair and shielded his upper face with his hands. The agony of having cancer was almost more than he could bear. But during the narration by Spencer of what had transpired down there came a different kind of pain, and a bitterness toward his wife. There was no question in his mind but that she had killed Navajo Killane. He had willed himself to believe that his woman was a no-account. The question now was who had been gunned down in that hotel room? According to Spencer, another man had shared the suite with Banner, a gambler, he'd said. As soon as someone had entered that room and turned on a lamp, the hands had blazed away, so it was entirely possible that Henry Banner was alive, had every right to head up here. Dammit, he was married to a bigamist! The thought stung, his anger bringing a surge of energy. And worse, a woman with blood on her hands.

"Tom, if Banner is alive he'll show up here. I want you to ride south, try to intercept the man."

"Then what, Mr. McClintock?"

"I don't want gunplay. Try to reason with the man."

"Should I tell him he ain't welcome here?"

"No . . . no . . . I must talk to him." McClintock waited until his segundo was gone, then he added, "Nothing has meaning anymore, Desmond."

"You said you wanted to see your son—"

McClintock's face brightened. "Bring Andy to me."

The study was in the west wing, and when the major-domo opened the door, he was certain he'd detected a moving shadow. Someone's been eavesdropping, he told himself, and by order of Casandra

McClintock. Ever since returning from Cheyenne the woman had confined herself to her room. Other than Jason McClintock, Desmond Parker was the only one who knew that Henry Banner had been Casandra's first husband. He would deal with this eavesdropping problem later.

The major-domo found Andrew Jason McClintock out behind the house, where he was being watched by one of the Mexican servants. He was fond of the boy, thought that Andy bore little resemblance to the rancher, something that he kept to himself. Seven, going on eight, Andy McClintock was large for his age, the mop of tousled brown hair covering his ears, and he had his mother's eyes, but they were in a longish face. "Come, Andy, your father wants to see you." He reached to stop the swing. After Parker had brought the boy to his father, he departed.

"Hiya, Pa."

"Hiya yourself, Andy." The boy started to climb into McClintock's lap, and he said, "Careful, son, these old bones ache some." When the boy had settled down, McClintock wrapped an arm around his son, let him snuggle against a bony shoulder.

"How come Ma didn't take me to Cheyenne?"

"Don't fret about it, son."

"Pa, when I grow up, I want to be a segundo. Then I can boss the men around like Tom does."

The joy of holding his son caused McClintock to release some of the anger he felt toward his wife, and he said softly, "When you grow up, Andy, you'll own the Mac spread. Running a cattle ranch is a lot of responsibility."

"Aw, Pa, it can't be that tough. You ever kill any

Injuns, Pa?"

"Oh," he murmured, "back a ways we had some troubles. One time . . ."

Casandra McClintock removed the ice pack from her forehead and dropped it on the floor. It rankled her that she'd been forced to leave most of her wardrobe behind. She should have used her head more, gone out on the town with the geologist, and by happenstance she could have run into the Mac hands, and— But this was all hindsight. At least she had finally gotten rid of her first husband.

Earlier, when her handmaid, Maria, had slipped up to inform her that her husband had sent for one of the hands who'd gone along to Cheyenne, she'd been terrified. On the return trip she'd told everyone to keep quiet about this, but some of them must have talked. On reflection, it would be her word against theirs. She would simply deny that she'd ordered them to kill Banner, saying that they were sent over to his hotel to make a citizen's arrest. Maybe this explanation wouldn't wash, but she'd be damned if she would admit to anything else.

When the knock came, she knew it was Maria, and Casandra eased out of bed and hurried to the door, and in broken English the Mexican woman told Casandra the gist of what she'd overheard Spencer tell those who were gathered with Jason McClintock.

"He can't be alive?"

"I am only repeating what Spencer said, Mrs. McClintock."

"Bring me some brandy!" Casandra lashed out, and

slammed the door behind the frightened woman. She began pacing the floor, fearing what would happen if Banner and the rancher got together and began comparing notes. If he was coming here, and a sudden instinct told her that he was, he must be waylaid. The only person she trusted to do that was the rancher's brother, Ox McClintock. Trusting, simple Ox must be aroused to anger, made to believe that Henry Banner was coming here to claim his son.

25

Long Henry knew he'd found the Mac spread when he came across some cattle carrying the Rocking MC brand. Looming majestically to the northwest were the Big Horns. A coyote stole out of a draw and seemed to spin around in midair when it discovered the horseman closing in, and ears laid back, the coyote made tracks for safer country. The grulla was bearing up well after the two day ride, not fighting the bit too much, and holding to a steady canter. Long Henry smoked as he rode, trying not to think too much about what lay ahead. He was still sickened by the death of Deacon O'Shay, a needless killing, one where some revenge must be exacted.

You don't gun down a woman. Given the opportunity, though, the heartless Casandra would sure as sin do him in. He rued the day when she came into his life. He would have been better off marrying an Apache squaw; Indian women stayed hair-tight to the wikiup and never lied.

The undulating prairie gave way to a series of draws cutting deep into the red-loamy earth, and where sagebrush and cactus intermingled, and on level stretches of land between and above antelope grazed. This was ambush country, and cautioned by that notion, he drew up and from force of habit checked his weapons over. A ranch this size would have thirty, forty riders, wind-weathered men who gave their boss a certain loyalty.

Ahead, a speck of dust grew larger, a mirage seeming to shimmer and dance until Long Henry could discern a lone rider. He was expecting company, but not someone off by his lonesome, and he urged his grulla on a converging course. When the distance closed to about a hundred yards, Long Henry stopped his horse and let the other rider come to him. He kept his hands folded over the saddle horn, smoke from his cigarette being tossed away by the quartering wind.

"I'm Tom Lamont, Jason McClintock's segundo," the man said without preamble, and Long Henry gazed with silent admiration at the purebred gelding the man rode.

"Henry Banner."

"Don't mind telling you, Banner, that I don't know what this is all about. Those hands who came back from Cheyenne told a pretty wild tale. But Jason McClintock wants to see you; and that's reason enough for me."

"I was expecting a different reception."

"Tell me true, Banner, did you gun down the breed?"

"Nope."

"As far as I'm concerned Killane was a sonofabitch. Well, you ready to ride?" The segundo swung his horse around and fell in to Long Henry's left, riding straight in the saddle, and with that sense of distance in his eyes that most cowpokes had.

"How far is it?"

"Seven miles as a crow flies."

They came to an arroyo, were forced to ride down the steep slope, find a crevice and let their horses move up toward the other rim. Nearing the top, the harsh report of a rifle was followed by an agonized neigh coming from the segundo's horse. The horse twisted sideways and fell against a brush pile, throwing Tom Lamont clear, and then it thrashed about before stiffening in death.

"Up there!" shouted Long Henry.

Further west and on the crest of the arroyo a man sat on a large dun-colored horse, and when the segundo clawed out his revolver and turned that way, he exclaimed angrily, "It's Ox!"

"So?" Long Henry brought his revolver to bear on the man.

"The boss's brother. But he didn't come here on his own. Mrs. McClintock had a hand in this."

Ducking behind the brush, Long Henry said, "Call him off, Lamont!"

"I'll try, but Ox is tetched in the head."

Another bullet fanned the air over their heads, and the segundo yelled out, "Ox, dammit, this is Tom Lamont! Hold your fire!"

"Tom, you're with a bad man," Ox hollered back. "He wants to take Andy away!"

"What in hell has that woman told him?"

"Most likely anything," responded Long Henry. "Take my horse. Try to work your way down the arroyo and come in from behind. It's me he's after. How big is he?"

"His pa could be a grizzly bear." Lamont led the grulla to the bottom of the arroyo, slid into the saddle and spurred hard to the west.

And above, Long Henry worked his way to the rim, shouted, "Any damn fool can bushwhack a man! Why don't we bare-knuckle one another." This should appeal to what pride the man had, he mused.

"I'll fight you!" Ox McClintock swung out of the saddle and dropped his rifle as he came along the edge of the arroyo.

Unbuckling his gun belt, Long Henry let it drop to the ground, and thinking maybe he'd made a mistake as he sized up Ox McClintock coming his way. Though he was of an equal height, or maybe a shade taller, the younger man was massive. He didn't seem to have any neck, only the large head pressing down on the solid trunk of rawhide and arms that reached to his knees. Get him mad, Long Henry said.

"Come on, you big ape!" he said tauntingly.

The blank eyes sparkled with anger before Ox McClintock broke into a run that carried him directly at his opponent. Sidestepping, Long Henry stuck out a boot and Ox went sprawling. He bounded up immediately, came again and with murderous intent. Long Henry shifted to his right, swung the other way, and clubbed the larger man as he blundered past.

"Like hitting a rock!" he mumbled. If Ox McClintock ever got him in a bear hug he'd be done for.

"Stand still!" Ox yelled.

·"Anyway you want it, ape!" He motioned the man to him, and when Ox did just that, Long Henry launched a vicious kick to the man's crotch.

Gasping in pain and doubling up, Ox clutched at

himself as he dropped to his knees, and stepping behind the man, Long Henry clamped his hands together and hit Ox behind the ear. Falling forward, Ox muttered, "Gonna get you . . ."

Long Henry backed off when he heard the segundo riding up, and then swung that way, fighting to get back his wind. "I'll tend to him," Lamont said. "Ride on ahead."

"I won't argue none there."

"Damn fool killed my horse. Deserves to walk back." The segundo nodded with his head toward the northwest. "Just keep heading toward Cloud Peak."

Thrusting a foot into the stirrup, he swung aboard the grulla and let it have its head. The brawl had served to relieve some of his nervous tension, and at least he knew that he wouldn't have to get through a gauntlet of angry cowhands. His left hand felt puffy, and he glanced at it. "Ox is all hat and no cattle."

26

"Are you sure about that?"

"Sí, Señor McClintock." The Mexican bowed and left.

McClintock said disbelievingly, "She's sending Ox to his death. What about that servant woman who was eavesdropping?"

"She'll be sent packing," the major-domo said, as he brought the wheelchair into the living room and turned it to face the open front door.

"Bring my wife to me, Desmond."

Desmond Parker went up the flight of stairs and to Casandra's bedroom, which he entered without bothering to knock.

"How dare you?"

"Your husband wants to see you."

Casandra emptied her glass, set it down on the vanity table and picked up the bottle of whiskey. "Not now."

"He knows that you sent Ox after Henry Banner."

She spun to him, eyes filled with hatred. "Look,

nigger, I will not be spoken to in that tone of voice. Tell him . . . tell him that I'll come down."

"As you say . . . bitch!" Parker threw her a cold smile and turned to go.

"Damn you!" Casandra shouted after him. Parker's insolence was going to cost him his job. And she'd get rid of the Mexican servants too. Moving to the dresser, she opened a drawer and lifted out her derringer. Ox would be no match for Henry Banner in a gunfight, but if Ox did get gunned down, it would remove another obstacle toward her inheriting the ranch upon the death of Jason McClintock. Before going to see Ox she'd changed into riding clothes, and now Casandra slipped the gun into a pocket and steeled herself with another half a glass of whiskey. She hadn't put on any makeup, wanting Jason to believe that she was still under a severe mental strain because of what had happened in Cheyenne.

"If only he'd die!" Then Casandra went out the door and toward that confrontation with her husband.

Upon stepping off the staircase, Casandra glanced at the front door standing open and beyond a ribbon of sunlight coming across the stained hardwood floor to a clear patch of sky showing above the outer stone wall encircling the house. Somewhere under that sky Ox could be lying dead by now. Solaced by this, she turned and went toward her husband sitting stoically in his wheelchair, a Mexican-style blanket covering his legs and lower body, while off to one side stood the ever-present major-domo.

"Jason," she said with a lightness she didn't feel, "you

211

look better, dear."

"Why did you do it?"

"Whatever do you mean?"

"Don't play games with me," he said tiredly. His eyes seemed larger than normal, the dominant feature in his skeletal face, and his hair had thinned so that a few liver spots could be seen on his glistening scalp. But in those eyes was an anger Casandra had never seen before.

"That man," she lashed out, "has never let go! Jason, you don't know how many letters I've gotten . . . threatening letters . . . saying what Banner will do when he gets me alone some place." She pulled out her handkerchief, dabbed at her eyes.

"Ox is no match for that man!" McClintock exploded. "But he means nothing to you, just someone you can use and discard. If my brother gets gunned down, I'm holding you personally responsible."

"Yes, yes, I sent Ox out there," she came back, "but only to tell Banner to go away. Why . . . I told Ox not to take a weapon along . . ."

"The hell you say," McClintock said grimly. "Then why did he borrow Rafael's rifle? And why did he keep telling Rafael that your former husband was coming here to take my son away?"

"I don't know what you're talking about—"

McClintock stiffened as a pain spasm shook his body, but with more of it seeming to be gathered in the area of his chest, that, and a bitter bile that filled his mouth. "Just what did happen down in Waco? You had me believe that your husband . . ."

"You're my husband."

"Am I? Getting back to Waco, the marshal there was more of a man than you led me to believe. I've made inquiries about Henry Banner. You lied to me about him . . . just as you've deceived me about your lover."

"Jason," she said, and moving toward him, "you're my husband. I love you, darling."

"Heaven help us, woman," he said, and with a sorrowing shake of his head, "you never got divorced from your first husband. That's why you sent my men after Banner down in Cheyenne. Probably one of the reasons you killed Navajo Killane."

"No, that isn't true!"

"You've even consorted with Killane in this house! Damn you, woman, you're a shameless hussy."

Casandra felt dizzy from the fear lodged in her mind, loathed the damning words being thrown at her by Jason McClintock. If Parker wasn't standing there, and damn him, sharing in her humiliation, she'd put a bullet through her husband's lying mouth. She heard the thudding of boots coming from outside, and she swung that way to see the Mexican, Rafael, coming up the walkway. The Mexican dashed inside, said loudly, "A rider is coming in, Señor McClintock . . . a stranger." Bowing, he backed to stand just outside the open door.

"No!" Casandra shouted hysterically. She pulled out the derringer. "You, Mexican, stand where Banner can see you. When he comes through the gate, wave him on in. You, nigger, my dear husband, stay where you are."

"I'll not have gunplay in my house."

"I'm giving the orders now, Jason dear! I've given you the best years of my life. I gave you a son. Now you won't stand behind me." Out of the corner of her eye Casandra saw the Mexican raising an arm to wave at whoever had arrived, and momentarily she forgot about the men in the living room.

Calmly, Jason McClintock pulled a corner of the blanket aside and picked up his worn Colt Dragoon. There was a strange buzzing in his head, and his heart seemed to be beating louder, the pain in his chest becoming more intense. He brought the barrel up, steadied the gun with both hands and said sharply, "Casandra!"

Reflexively, she half-turned, with her eyes glazing in shock when she saw the gun, the intention of what he was going to do planted on his face, and too late she started to swing her own gun in his direction. The gun bucked in McClintock's hand. The slug took her in the stomach, and she staggered sideways, held out an entreating hand. "I'm doing this . . . for us . . . Jason dear . . ." She died then, crumpling gracefully, and lay there while still clutching the derringer.

Desmond Parker's eyes had been centered on the woman, and even now with the sound of the gun still ringing in his ears he couldn't believe that Jason McClintock would kill his own wife. Then he became aware of the rancher slumped to one side in the wheelchair.

"Mr. McClintock?" he said, stepping around the wheelchair. He placed a hand at the man's temple;

there was no pulse beat. He realized the rancher had died from a broken heart or what had been consuming him. Quickly he took the gun out of McClintock's hand and tossed it on the floor some distance away. On the front porch, Rafael moved to stand framed in the open doorway. "What happened here is between us."

"Sí, Señor Parker, between us."

Out beyond the encircling stone wall, Long Henry had seen the Mexican waving to him as he rode up, and now he spun away from the tie rail when he heard the bark of a handgun. He palmed his revolver and went through the open gate and along the fieldstone walkway. The Mexican removed his wide-brimmed sombrero and stepped aside as Long Henry passed him. Beyond the patch of sunlight on the floor Long Henry looked hard at the black man standing by the wheelchair, then lowered his eyes to the body lying on the floor. He holstered his gun.

"I believe she's dead," Parker intoned.

Entering, he moved to stand by the body. "Reckon she is." Gazing down at her now, it was as if he were viewing the remains of a stranger. But somehow he felt cleansed, yet drained. "The rancher, did she gun him down?"

"Mr. McClintock died from a broken heart."

Long Henry focused his attention on the revolver that the major-domo had discarded, wanting to ask who had killed Casandra, knowing that no answer would be forthcoming. It had been a long ride up here from Cheyenne, and he was tired, or maybe this great weariness came from searching for her all these years.

"We must talk."

"About what?"

"There's something you must know," said Desmond Parker.

27

"The moment you came through that door I knew you were the boy's father."

"I didn't know she was with child down there."

Desmond Parker wore a plain black suit, having just come from where they'd buried Jason McClintock and his wife. The only ones in attendance had been the Mac hands, the servants, and Henry Banner. Ox McClintock had been there too, and the rancher's son. The boy's presence had disturbed Long Henry more than he realized, and with these spoken words of Parker's he knew the answer to his puzzlement.

"Jason McClintock was a respected man in these parts, Mr. Banner. The truth of what happened yesterday will stay here."

"I've no objections to that."

"Now, to the boy," he said uncertainly. "Mr. McClintock willed everything to his son. He loved Andy. More than you realize, Mr. Banner. Especially after he found out about his wife and Killane."

Long Henry glanced around the living room at the many western and Spanish artifacts, and impressed by the house itself. He could never give his son something like this, nor a respected name. He'd become a gambler, a drifter, someone without roots or too much possibles to speak of. Besides, he knew nothing about rearing a young one. Andy's ties were here, as was his fortune, Long Henry figured.

"The boy won't hear it from me that I'm his pa." Long Henry rose. "Time to head out, I reckon."

Desmond Parker walked with Long Henry to the tie rail outside the wall, where he said, "Andy's made of tough fiber. When the time is right, I think it only proper that he learn who his real father is. What happened here yesterday, I trust that will be forgotten."

"Best that way." Long Henry untied the reins, turned wondering eyes back to Parker. "You really think the boy . . . my son . . . would look with favor on me once he finds out?"

"He'll be raised proper, Mr. Banner. Come back when he's got fuzz on his chin and is eyeing some young fillies."

"Might just do that." He held out his hand, which Desmond Parker grasped. "You know, Mr. Parker, you should have been a lawyer."

Parker laughed. "Helping out here is about all I can handle for now. Adios, my friend."

When Long Henry reached the upper reaches beyond the flood basin, he slouched in the saddle and gave the Big Horns a studious look. Eastward were the Black Hills and a desirable woman, and that ranch O'Shay had deeded to him. Somehow he wasn't ready for something permanent. Somehow he wanted to ride in to new territory, see what lay beyond those mountains, and he'd heard that silver had been found up in Coeur D'Alene country.

"Well, hoss, let's mosey on . . . find a campsite before nightfall."

Digging his spurs into the flanks of the grulla, he rode on toward the beckoning mystery of the mountains, and smiling at the song of a meadowlark as he cantered across a meadow spangled with flowers, knowing that after all these years he was a free creature too.

ACTION ADVENTURE

SILENT WARRIORS (1675, $3.95)
by Richard P. Henrick
The Red Star, Russia's newest, most technologically advanced submarine, outclasses anything in the U.S. fleet. But when the captain opens his sealed orders 24 hours early, he's staggered to read that he's to spearhead a massive nuclear first strike against the Americans!

THE PHOENIX ODYSSEY (1789, $3.95)
by Richard P. Henrick
All communications to the USS *Phoenix* suddenly and mysteriously vanish. Even the urgent message from the president cancelling the War Alert is not received. In six short hours the *Phoenix* will unleash its nuclear arsenal against the Russian mainland.

COUNTERFORCE (2013, $3.95)
Richard P. Henrick
In the silent deep, the chase is on to save a world from destruction. A single Russian Sub moves on a silent and sinister course for American shores. The men aboard the U.S.S. *Triton* must search for and destroy the Soviet killer Sub as an unsuspecting world races for the apocalypse.

EAGLE DOWN (1644, $3.75)
by William Mason
To western eyes, the Russian Bear appears to be in hibernation — but half a world away, a plot is unfolding that will unleash its awesome, deadly power. When the Russian Bear rises up, God help the Eagle.

DAGGER (1399, $3.50)
by William Mason
The President needs his help, but the CIA wants him dead. And for Dagger — war hero, survival expert, ladies man and mercenary extraordinaire — it will be a game played for keeps.

Available wherever paperbacks are sold, or order direct from the Publisher. Send cover price plus 50¢ per copy for mailing and handling to Zebra Books, Dept. 2155, 475 Park Avenue South, New York, N.Y. 10016. Residents of New York, New Jersey and Pennsylvania must include sales tax. DO NOT SEND CASH.

SWEET MEDICINE'S PROPHECY
by Karen A. Bale

#1: SUNDANCER'S PASSION (1778, $3.95)

Stalking Horse was the strongest and most desirable of the tribe, and Sun Dancer surrounded him with her spell-binding radiance. But the innocence of their love gave way to passion—and passion, to betrayal. Would their relationship ever survive the ultimate sin?

#2: LITTLE FLOWER'S DESIRE (1779, $3.95)

Taken captive by savage Crows, Little Flower fell in love with the enemy, handsome brave Young Eagle. Though their hearts spoke what they could not say, they could only dream of what could never be. . . .

#3: WINTER'S LOVE SONG (1780, $3.95)

The dark, willowy Anaeva had always desired just one man: the half-breed Trenton Hawkins. But Trenton belonged to two worlds—and was torn between two women. She had never failed on the fields of war; now she was determined to win on the battle-ground of love!

#4: SAVAGE FURY (1768, $3.95)

Aeneva's rage knew no bounds when her handsome mate Trent commanded her to tend their tepee as he rode into danger. But under cover of night, she stole away to be with Trent and share whatever perils fate dealt them.

#5: SUN DANCER'S LEGACY (1878, $3.95)

Aeneva's and Trenton's adopted daughter Anna becomes the light of their lives. As she grows into womanhood, she falls in love with blond Steven Randall. Together they discover the secrets of their passion, the bitterness of betrayal—and fight to fulfill the prophecy that is Anna's birthright.

THE UNTAMED WEST
brought to you by Zebra Books

THE LAST MOUNTAIN MAN　　　　　　　　(1480, $2.25)
by William W. Johnstone

He rode out West looking for the men who murdered his father and brother. When an old mountain man taught him how to kill a man a hundred different ways from Sunday, he knew he'd make sure they all remembered . . . THE LAST MOUNTAIN MAN.

SAN LOMAH SHOOTOUT　　　　　　　　(1853, $2.50)
by Doyle Trent

Jim Kinslow didn't even own a gun, but a group of hardcases tried to turn him into buzzard meat. There was only one way to find out why anybody would want to stretch his hide out to dry, and that was to strap on a borrowed six-gun and ride to death or glory.

TOMBSTONE LODE　　　　　　　　(1915, $2.95)
by Doyle Trent

When the Josey mine caved in on Buckshot Dobbs, he left behind a rich vein of Colorado gold—but no will. James Alexander, hired to investigate Buckshot's self-proclaimed blood relations learns too soon that he has one more chance to solve the mystery and save his skin or become another victim of TOMBSTONE LODE.

GALLOWS RIDERS　　　　　　　　(1934, $2.50)
by Mark K. Roberts

When Stark and his killer-dogs reached Colby, all it took was a little muscle and some well-placed slugs to run roughshod over the small town—until the avenging stranger stepped out of the shadows for one last bloody showdown.

DEVIL WIRE　　　　　　　　(1937, $2.50)
by Cameron Judd

They came by night, striking terror into the hearts of the settlers. The message was clear: Get rid of the devil wire or the land would turn red with fencestringer blood. It was the beginning of a brutal range war.

Available wherever paperbacks are sold, or order direct from the Publisher. Send cover price plus 50¢ per copy for mailing and handling to Zebra Books, Dept. 2155, 475 Park Avenue South, New York, N.Y. 10016. Residents of New York, New Jersey and Pennsylvania must include sales tax. DO NOT SEND CASH.